## "You can start by taking off your clothes."

"Pardon me?" Nate asked.

Tamara's cheeks blushed a vivid pink, but she looked him right in the eye. "You asked what you can do for me and...I think, I hope, that I haven't been wildly off the mark with you being attracted to me."

He nodded. "Yeah." It was an understatement, but he wasn't exactly at his best at the moment. In fact, he might have just had a small stroke.

"Since the odds of us living long, happy lives is about one in a million, I think we should do whatever we can in whatever time we have that brings us pleasure." She patted the spot beside her on the bed.

Nate ought to have some kind of reasonable argument. He was the team leader. He was responsible for her, for all of them. Having sex would complicate things.

But all he kept thinking was *thank you, thank you....*

# Blaze™

Dear Reader,

I first learned about Nate Pratchett in a dream I had almost two years ago. He came to me angry and all he wanted was revenge. At the time, I saw him clearly, as if he'd been a friend from long ago, one who'd meant a lot to me but had disappeared from my life.

Nate in my dreams was the genesis of the whole IN TOO DEEP... miniseries, and he was pretty insistent about how he wanted things to go. But I knew there was more to Nate's life than being the good soldier.

It was time for Nate to have his own reckoning. And more important, it was time for Nate to find love. Despite the danger. Despite the hopelessness of the moment. In the end, he fought as hard for his happiness, for his love, as he did for his freedom.

It was a worthwhile lesson for both of us.

Love,

*Jo Leigh*

P.S. Please visit my Web site www.joleigh.com for information on upcoming titles and more!

# RECKONING

## JO LEIGH

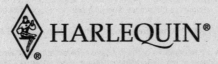

TORONTO • NEW YORK • LONDON
AMSTERDAM • PARIS • SYDNEY • HAMBURG
STOCKHOLM • ATHENS • TOKYO • MILAN • MADRID
PRAGUE • WARSAW • BUDAPEST • AUCKLAND

ISBN-13: 978-0-373-79317-4
ISBN-10:     0-373-79317-0

RECKONING

## ABOUT THE AUTHOR

Jo Leigh has written over thirty novels for Harlequin and Silhouette Books since 1994. She's a double RITA® Award finalist, and was part of the Harlequin Blaze launch. She also teaches writing in workshops across the country.

Jo lives in Utah with her wonderful husband and their new puppy, Jessie. You can chat with her at her Web site, www.joleigh.com, and don't forget to check out her daily blog!

### Books by Jo Leigh
HARLEQUIN BLAZE
   2—GOING FOR IT!
  23—SCENT OF A WOMAN
  34—SENSUAL SECRETS
  72—A DASH OF TEMPTATION
  88—TRUTH OR DARE
122—ARM CANDY
134—THE ONE WHO GOT AWAY
165—A LICK AND A PROMISE
178—HUSH
227—MINUTE BY MINUTE
265—CLOSER..
289—RELENTLESS*
301—RELEASE*

*In Too Deep...

To Birgit, for all the wonderful support.
It's been thrilling.

# CAST OF CHARACTERS

*Nate Pratchett:* Delta Force Commander—leader of the team, wanted for treason

*Tamara Chen:* Biochemist—tricked into creating a nightmare; forced to live a life underground...till now

*Seth Turner:* Delta Force Surveillance—lost his hand, but healed by the love of Harper

*Harper Douglas:* Physician—eyewitness to the scope of Omicron's weapon

*Boone Ferguson:* Delta Force Communications—risked his life to save his best friend's sister, Christie

*Christie Pratchett:* Innocent Bystander—lost her old life, but found hope and love with Boone

*Kate Rydell:* Forensic Accountant—the first to realize Omicron's plan

*Vince Yarrow:* L.A. Homicide Detective—turned in his badge to fight for his woman, Kate

*Cade Huston:* Delta Force Sniper—lived silently and alone while he fought for the team and the girl he left behind

*Eli Lieberman:* Cub Reporter for the *L.A. Times*—willing to risk everything to report the truth

*Leland Ingram:* CEO of Omicron—the man in charge of death

*Jackson Raines:* Senator and guiding force behind Omicron

*Omicron:* A rogue CIA operation whose goal is to sell an illegal, toxic chemical weapon to the highest bidders and use the money for political gain

# *Prologue*

ELI LIEBERMAN STARED AT the notebook in his hand, afraid to open it. He checked his front door again to make sure all the locks were in place, but what were locks? *They* could get past locks.

Taking a deep breath, he sat down at his kitchen table. The day had been long and frustrating. Every single lead he'd pursued on this story had dried up. No one would talk to him. The only thing he could do now was to go back to the beginning. Corky Baker's notes.

Well, they'd become *his* notes after he'd found Baker dead. Baker had been the number one investigative journalist at the *Los Angeles Times,* while he'd just been a glorified fact checker.

He stared at it again, a small lined notebook with a blue cover. They sold for less than a buck. But inside this particular notebook was information that had already gotten one man killed, and if Eli transcribed the notes, could very likely lead to his own death.

Shit. He was only twenty-three.

He put the notebook in his briefcase, the one he'd gotten from his Uncle Morty when he'd graduated from college. Of course Uncle Morty had also told him he was a schmuck for wanting to be a reporter, that all it would bring him was headaches and overdue bills, and what girl in her right mind would want to marry a man with no money?

After a few minutes of agonizing indecision, he snatched the notebook out, but this time, Eli flipped it open to the first page. Hell, he shouldn't be so edgy about transcribing the notes. He was already doomed. He couldn't end up *more* dead. The bad guys from Omicron already knew about him and that, according to Vince Yarrow, was enough. And Vince should know—he was an L.A. homicide detective. No. Used to be. Now he worked with Nate Pratchett. Who was wanted for treason. Who led a team of ex-Delta Force soldiers, a biochemist, a doctor and an accountant, all of them on the run, all of them being hunted by the rogue CIA agents working for Omicron, all of them in possession of secrets that would turn the world of U.S. politics on its ass…. Then there was the matter of a deadly gas that could wipe people out. Big time.

He might as well transcribe the damn notes.

It probably would have been easier if it hadn't been almost midnight. If he hadn't been sitting in the chair that squeaked, and if he'd turned on more lights.

No, he could do this. Just reading the notebook would not put a curse on his head. It only felt as if it would.

Eli flipped open the book, squinting as he tried to decipher the almost illegible scrawl that was Corky Baker's handwriting. Any normal person would have tossed the notebook in the trash thinking it was nonsense.

But after having transcribed some of Baker's other stories, Eli was familiar with Baker's unique shorthand.

As he deciphered the first page, then the second, his heart beat faster, and all he wanted in this world was to write it all down. Yeah, he'd give Baker the credit, at least for the first part of the story.

As for the ending? It didn't look good for Nate and the other fugitives. They were fighting big power and big money, and they had neither.

That's what had made Baker pursue the story in the first place. It had all the earmarks of David versus Goliath, although it was clear Baker thought Goliath was gonna win hands down.

Eli wasn't so sure.

# 1

NATE PRATCHETT stared down into hell, watching the underground lab burn. They'd found Tam. They'd either killed or taken her, and both options made him sick to his stomach. If they'd found Tam, he had to assume they'd found them all. As he was standing here, they might be at Kate and Vince's, at his place where Cade was going over recordings from the bugs placed in the office Omicron used as a front in downtown L.A. All his friends might be dead.

He stepped back as the heat intensified, and that was lucky because something down in the lab exploded, rocking the building around him. He had to get out of here, now, before the whole place came down.

The complex itself had been an incredible find, but there had always been inherent danger. Built by Colombian drug dealers, it had been an underground labyrinth of rooms and escape routes. He'd turned it into a lab for Tam, who'd been a virtual prisoner there during the past two years as she'd worked on the antidote for the deadly gas created by Omicron. Now it was ashes and the end of hope.

There was only one chance that she wasn't dead or

captured, but he hesitated. If she wasn't there… No, he had to go. Had to know. If she had made it out, she was probably hurt.

That thought spurred him into a run. He was halfway down the block before it occurred to him that he was heading straight for the Plan B building, and that Omicron might be watching him.

It wasn't like him to be so careless, but shit, *Tam.*

He darted into an abandoned building nearby and pressed himself against a wall while his eyes grew accustomed to the dark. It was one of the many ramshackle buildings in the projects of East Los Angeles that had once housed the poor. Even they'd moved on, except for those too whacked-out on drugs or alcohol, or who thought they could still make a buck. Mostly rats lived there. Rats and packs of dogs.

He could see now—shapes at least. There were almost no working street lights here. The city had stopped replacing them. Which made it an excellent hiding space, but damned hard to negotiate without a flashlight.

One thing in his favor, and hopefully Tam's, was that they'd gone over this route over and over again. He'd wanted her to be able to find her way in the pitch-black night. He'd wanted her safe.

IN DARKNESS SO BLACK IT FELT like blindness, Tamara Chen touched her eyes to see if they were open. The gun in her other hand shook from her trembling, making her feel useless and petrified.

She'd just killed a man.

He'd been alive one second and dead the next, and it didn't seem to matter that he'd tried to kill her. She'd pulled the trigger. The recoil had knocked her against the wall of the lab and hurt her wrist, but even so she'd shot him in the head. A fluke, an accident. One that had saved her life.

She curled her arm around her body, but it did nothing against the frigid January air. She'd left her coat. Her cell phone had been destroyed, along with her clothes, her pictures, her journals. Everything she had was now gone except the clothes she wore and the flash drive that hung on a long chain around her neck.

The last five years of her life were stored in it, and she could go to any computer, plug it in the USB port and there it would be. Formulas, notes, test results. Failures.

The last two weeks in the lab had been a new kind of hell for her. Nothing she'd experienced before, whether in school or at work, had prepared her for a failure of such magnitude. What in hell had made her think she could save the day? She was a biochemist. A good one. But she'd fallen so short of the mark on this one—

A sound, the crack of a branch? A backfire in the distance? She lifted the gun again, still shaking as badly as when she'd first planted herself in the corner.

They'd found her. Omicron had found her. They were clever bastards, but she'd been so careful. She never made phone calls, except with the clean cell phones Nate gave her. She hid in the basement lab, having her groceries and supplies brought to her rather than risk a trip to the market.

Nothing in her life, ever since she'd returned to the States from Kosovo, had been normal. Even her Internet connection, which she used only when absolutely necessary, had been routed through so many blind alleys and foreign ports that it would take a genius months—if ever—to pinpoint her location.

So what had gone wrong? Had they found Nate? Followed him?

The thought filled her with a whole new level of terror. If Nate had been captured, if he was dead, then she might as well give it up. There would be no winning if Nate was out of the picture. Since day one, he'd been the leader.

The first time she'd met him she'd been in Serbia, in a cramped lab, working on the development of a new chemical compound.

That seemingly dream job had come to her out of the blue. She'd just finished her final doctoral thesis and had scored a plum position working for her chemistry professor, Dr. Brennan. But Brennan had introduced her to a man claiming to be working on a secret government project. He'd offered her two hundred thousand dollars for two years of work, if she was willing to relocate to Kosovo. She wasn't told what the project was, only her part.

While she'd known several of the other scientists who'd been approached, mostly chemists like herself, she'd had to sign a non-fraternization contract, as well as a nondisclosure agreement. One slip of the tongue, and there would be no payoff. She'd gotten a weekly per diem that took care of her necessities, and they'd provided housing, but the big money was all due upon completion. She used to spend hours at night, planning how she'd spend her two hundred grand.

How jumping on that incredible opportunity had led her to being hunted down by a rogue CIA unit was still beyond her comprehension. Those men from Omicron had destroyed the lab, trashed her personal belongings and tried to kidnap—if not kill—her. Her. Tamara Chen. Who'd been a science nerd since grade school. Who used to look forward to music night with her Mom and Dad. Who'd gone out on her first date at eighteen. Who'd never been in love.

She froze as another crack sounded. This time it wasn't far away, and this time it was followed by foot-steps coming closer, walking through the condemned building toward her.

Somehow she managed to get to her feet, then she pointed the gun in front of herself. She had no idea if she was aiming at a wall or a torn-up couch, but she had to do something. She didn't want to die, not at twenty-eight. It was the most terrified she'd ever been, and in the last few years, she'd been shaken a lot.

She'd anxiously brooded about this moment, what it would be like to come face to face with the shadowy men of Omicron determined to kill her and her friends because of their discovery of Omicron's deadly plans while they were stationed in Kosovo. It sucked.

NATE MOVED MORE CAREFULLY, uncomfortably aware that if Omicron was watching, they'd be using infrared. The only way to get where he needed to go was to use the buildings themselves as cover.

One room at a time, one wall at a time, he made his way block by block. He was getting closer, and his heart beat hard and heavy in his chest, dreading what he would find.

He finally reached the building, the one they'd chosen as a fail-safe. She was behind that wall or she wasn't, and he'd have to deal with it. That's all. He could do this.

One step, then another. The darkness here was total and there was no choice but to reach into his back pocket and take out his penlight. He looked away, turned on the thing, then followed the beam of light around the corner.

It was Tam. Bloody, shaking so hard her weapon was all over the map and filthy, but it was Tam and she was alive.

"Stop or I'll shoot," she said, her voice quavering, her eyes shut tight against the light.

"It's me," Nate said, and he had to repeat it because his voice broke. "Tam, it's me."

She stilled for a moment, then opened her eyes. "Nate?"

She sounded like a child. A frightened, desperate child.

He holstered his gun and crossed the distance between them. Gently pushing aside her weapon, he took her in his arms. "It's okay," he said, his words muffled on her hair. "I'm here."

She dropped her gun on the floor and clutched his back. He felt her sob before he heard it, her whole chest heaving against him.

"Shh," he said, rocking her. "Are you hurt?"

She shook her head.

"Can you walk?"

A nod.

"Okay, baby, let's take it slowly. I want to make sure there's no one out there."

She sniffed, then drew her head back. "I killed him," she said.

"That was good. You did great."

"He pointed his gun at me, but I shot first. There was no time."

"You did the right thing," he said. She was freaked, and he got that. Ordinary people freaked about death. About killing. They weren't trained for anything else. "He was a bad guy, so don't sweat it. Right now, we have to get out of here. They could come back."

She hung on to him as he bent for her gun. He could feel her body tremble as he led her on a circuitous route through what was left of the building. It took a lot longer to get back to his truck than it had to get to her. They kept the light out for most of the journey, and toward the end she had slowed to a crawl, but finally they were in the truck and on their way.

He'd decided where to take her as they'd walked through buildings, so he knew to get on the freeway toward the San Fernando Valley. She sat close, resting her head on his shoulder.

He would have put his arm around her if he hadn't been so worried about the rest of the team. Although it hurt him to bother her, he had her shift so he could get his cell, a new one that couldn't be traced, and dialed Kate and Vince.

"Hello?" Kate murmured sleepily.

He had no idea what time it was, just that it was late. "Tam's been compromised," he said.

There was silence on the phone and when Kate said, "Where do you want us?" she didn't sound in the least bit sleepy now.

"Meet up with Seth and Boone. We'll follow."

Kate hung up, but Nate knew two things. One, that she and Vince were alive, and two, that they would be out of their rented house in an hour, on their way to Nevada.

He dialed Cade's phone. Being the soldier he was, he knew the drill, too. Only he'd have to pack Nate's stuff as well as his own, and since Nate had the truck, he'd have to find some other transportation.

As Nate drove onto the 101 Freeway, he dialed his sister's cell. As he'd expected, Boone and Seth were out on recon, but Christie assured him that no one had been snooping around. She promised to be vigilant and discuss the situation with the guys as soon as they returned. Harper, a doctor who'd also been in Kosovo and joined their cause, was out pulling double duty on her waitressing job.

The four of them were staying in a ratty motel in a tiny town just outside of Nellis Air Force Base. They'd wired the place like Fort Knox, so if anyone had been asking about them, they'd most likely know it. If they had the least bit of doubt, they'd pack and leave.

He got onto Ventura Boulevard then glanced at Tamara. She was sleeping, her lips slightly parted, her face smudged with dirt. Probably blood, too, but it was dark, so he didn't have to think about that. Somehow, she still managed to look innocent.

He put the phone on the dash so he could shift her into a more comfortable position, but he picked it up again as he remembered one more call that couldn't wait, even if it meant waking Tam.

He dialed Eli Lieberman. He was just a kid, a junior reporter for the *L.A. Times,* but he'd taken up their cause and was willing to run with it. Nate wasn't sure if he was braver than hell or just nuts. The last reporter who'd tried to help them had been buried several weeks ago.

But Eli had insisted, and Nate had taken him into the fold. The kid didn't answer right away, and after the phone switched to voice mail, Nate hung up and dialed again. He did that two more times, then heard Eli's groggy voice.

"You okay?"

"What? Who the hell is this?"

"It's Nate."

"Oh, shit. Why?"

"One of the team was compromised. I wanted to make sure they hadn't found you."

"Oh, shit," he repeated, more fully awake.

"You have your weapon?"

"Yeah, but I can't hit the side of a barn door."

"You don't have to. You stick the gun in your assailant's stomach and pull the trigger. Easy as pie."

"I don't know how to bake, either."

"I think you're in the clear." Nate turned on Sycamore, then on Vanowen. "If they were going to go after you, they'd have been there by now. Just keep an eye out."

"As if I'll ever sleep again."

"We're changing our base of operations. I'll call you in a day or two."

"Are you leaving the city?"

"More than that. I have to go. Stay safe." Just as Nate was hanging up, he heard Eli's, "Oh, shit," one last time.

There was the hotel. It wasn't one he'd usually choose. This place had an elevator and room service. It also had a great big bathtub and beds soft as a cloud. His only problem was going to be getting Tam up to the room. He'd use the service elevator, but he hadn't checked out the place and he wasn't sure where it was.

He turned the truck into the underground parking, and his problem was solved almost instantly. There was a delivery truck by the restaurant back door, and Nate could see the service elevator right inside.

He parked close to the exit, and as the truck's motor cut off, Tam woke. She blinked, looked around. "Where are we?"

"Hotel. I'm going to get a room, but you'll need to stay in the truck while I do it."

She looked at him with terrified eyes, but she nodded. He handed her the Glock she'd dropped back at the fail-safe, and she had enough wits about her to check the safety. "Go. I'll keep low."

He smiled at her, wanting to do more. Instead, he opened his door.

"Wait."

He turned back.

She reached up and wiped his temple with the flat of her thumb. "Ash."

He got out of the truck before he did something stupid. Like kiss her. Not that wanting to do that was anything new. But it still wasn't right. He was responsible for her safety. How could she trust him if he came onto her? So he didn't. Even though he wanted her as fervently as his old life.

By the time he'd spent too much on a room and returned to the car, Tam was trembling again. He'd known it would be difficult for her, but he hadn't realized the desk clerk would move like molasses. Tam had cleaned her face a bit, but there was no way to get her in through the lobby.

There was no one near the delivery truck, so he did a very brief check, then practically carried her into the service elevator.

Though he had his gun at the ready, he doubted he'd need it. He'd know if they had been followed. At least, he had to believe that or go insane.

No one was in the hallway on the sixth floor, and he could see the relief on her face, in her body, as they entered the privacy of the room. He bolted the door, then led her to the edge of the big, king-sized bed. "I asked for two queens, but this is all they had left."

She sat down, looking as if she'd fall over in a stiff breeze. "That's good," she said. "I want you to sleep with me."

He felt his body tighten but kept his reaction from his face. "Sure. No problem. We'll just get you in the tub first."

She didn't even nod or look at him. All she did was close her eyes, and he wondered if she was going to make it through a bath.

What he knew for sure is that he wouldn't be getting any sleep. He headed for the bathroom, and as he started the water in the big tub, he whispered, "Oh, shit."

# 2

BOONE FERGUSON HELD THE door open for Seth, then followed him inside the lion's den. It was late—the graveyard shift here at Omicron's Nevada plant—and they were dressed in blue coveralls like all the other people showing up to work. They'd stolen the uniforms three nights ago. It had taken them awhile to make their badges look legitimate. There was no reason for anyone to stop them, to question them. Unless they blew it.

All it would take was one false step and it would be over for both of them. If they were discovered, they had their instructions. No surrender. No interrogation. Period.

Boone had been a soldier for a long time and the possibility of death came with the territory. Only now, for the first time in his life, he cared. One hell of a lot.

He didn't want to leave Christie. The thought of never seeing her again made him gut sick. He'd only just found her. In a goddamn crummy way, that's for sure, but he figured that had helped them get closer.

Months earlier she'd been stalked to the point of abandoning her home and any life she'd known. At Nate's request, Boone had gone to help. He'd fallen for her hard, even though he didn't want her to be involved in this Omicron mess. It had thrown both of them when they'd discovered the stalker was actually an Omicron agent, looking for Nate. She'd been targeted, just like the rest of them. So they'd joined forces, and he'd never have guessed how it could change his life.

The irony wasn't lost on him. He thought often about the Dickens' quote, "It was the best of times…" Being with Christie was the best thing that had ever happened to him. Being a fugitive because of Omicron's lies was the worst.

Tonight, he and Seth were going to be risking more than on any other foray. They were going inside, to map out the plant as thoroughly as possible. Although they hadn't figured out what, exactly, they were going to do with the information, it was important to know what they were up against.

So they walked inside the cavernous room, filled with production lines and heavy machinery. This wasn't where they made the deadly gas. It was where they made the canisters. On the surface, an innocuous enough task for the employee.

Walking quickly down one side of the long building, Boone estimated there were around seventy people in this room alone. He'd seen the parking lot, but he'd underestimated the number of employees who were bused here from Vegas and Mesquite.

The number of people who dealt directly with the gas would be small in comparison. For all Boone knew, they only did the most dangerous work on the day shift in another part of the factory. They'd have to keep exploring if they wanted to know for sure.

He looked ahead at Seth, who he knew was memorizing the layout for the moment they were free. Seth's prosthetic hand was in his coverall pocket. He'd lost his hand in an earlier skirmish with Omicron, but Harper had saved his life. And there was more going on there. Boone grinned.

Seth led him past a large break room. There were rows of tables and benches and the walls were lined with vending machines. Two big refrigerators were in the back, along with a row of microwaves.

Next, they went past a locker room, and it was crowded. Men and women were stowing lunches or purses into their lockers, and he saw a number of them putting on hairnets. Like most workplaces, there was a smattering of laughter and a lot of talk. No one took notice of him or Seth.

Finally, they reached a door that held promise. A woman walked in, using a keycard. He only caught a glimpse, but it was enough to make him curse. There was a biometric hand scanner inside, one that read fingerprints. How the hell were they going to get past that device?

He moved on, following the wall until he got to the back door. A loud alarm rang, and his heart pounded until he realized it was just the work horn. The graveyard shift had officially started.

He pushed open the door and found Seth waiting. They headed toward building two where they'd find a bathroom, lock themselves inside stalls and diagram the production line. Then they'd go through the whole exercise again, until just before dawn.

One more time, they'd race across the desert until they reached the hole in the fence. One more time, Boone would pray they wouldn't be spotted by the security guards in the air, in the jeeps, monitoring the surveillance cameras. All he had to do was keep his eye on the goal. A lifetime with Christie where they didn't have to hide. Where they didn't have to be scared. Where they could finally be free.

SHE WANTED TO SLEEP FOREVER, but Tam forced herself to sit on the edge of the bed as she waited for Nate. The bath would take more energy than she had, but more than anything she needed to wash away the remnants that clung to her skin, her hair, and under her nails from what had happened tonight.

The sound of water filling the tub lulled her even closer to sleep, and she jerked up, almost falling over.

Nate walked out of the bathroom, his jacket off, his blue chambray shirtsleeves rolled above his elbows. He smiled so warmly, she managed a smile back. She only wished she could stop shaking.

"It's ready."

She nodded as she stood, then looked back at the bedspread. She expected to see more ash and dirt on the clean white comforter, but it wasn't too bad. Just a couple of smudges.

"You okay?"

He stood right next to her and she leaned against him as she'd done in the car. "I'm so tired."

"That's shock. I'm worried that you're going to fall asleep in the tub."

She yawned, not even covering her mouth. Her mother would have scolded her for that, although not until they were in private. "I probably will."

He put his hand on her waist, gripping strongly. "Maybe we should skip it. Or put you in the shower."

"No. Just come with me. If I start to drown, pull me up by the hair."

He didn't answer, and his hand tightened further on her waist. She should look at him, see what was going on, but screw it. She had to get clean. As tired as she was, sleeping in her own filth held no appeal. The very idea made her skin crawl. "Come on. Let's do it."

He helped her into the large bathroom, and for a moment she felt disoriented. The white tile, the white towels. Everything was clean and bright. This was the real world. The kind of place she'd dreamed about in her long stay underground.

He guided her over to the commode and after he put the seat down, he seated her. "We have to get these off," he said. His voice sounded strange, or maybe it was her ears. She wouldn't trust anything tonight.

He lifted her arms and pulled the T-shirt over her head. She felt no embarrassment being in her bra. Or out of it. Being naked was the least of her problems. If it had been anyone else, she probably would have been more concerned, but it was Nate, and his hands were so big and so gentle. He removed her clothes as if she were a child. Lifting one foot, then the other to take off her shoes. He stood her up to get her jeans off. Smart man, he took her panties along with them.

When he had her in the buff, he walked her over to

the tub and held on to her as she got in the hot water. It took a minute for her to adjust to the temperature, but he was patient. Quiet, too. Inch by inch she lay down, letting the warmth seep deep into her bones.

When she was up to her neck in water, she looked up at Nate. He wasn't smiling, in fact, his lips were pressed so tightly together they were white. She would have asked him what was wrong, but her head went back and her eyes shut as she tried to let the horrors of the night go…for now.

She felt him sit on the edge of the tub, and she giggled with the thought that he was the best bath toy ever. Rubber ducks included. She must be losing it.

"What's so funny?"

"Nothing."

"Okay. Uh, you want me to put some soap on the washcloth for you?"

"Sure, why not?"

He reached over her and grabbed the bar of hotel soap and then he dipped the cloth in the water. "I'll bet you're a real fun drunk."

"I wouldn't know," she said. "I've never been drunk."

"Never? Not even in college?"

"Nope."

"Come on. I've met guys from MIT. They partied as hard as anyone."

"I was too busy being a nerd," she said. "I didn't have a social life."

"I can't picture that," he said as he leaned toward her. He pushed her hair back with his tender touch, then slowly cleaned her face with the soft cloth. "I'll bet every guy in Cambridge was banging at your door."

"You'd lose your money."

"You didn't have a boyfriend?"

"One. But he was a bigger nerd than I was. We spent all our time in the lab. We never even did it."

His hand stilled. She could just imagine the shocked look on his face. One thing for sure, no one would ever call Nate a nerd. He was everything women swoon over—tall, dark, handsome as sin. Those green eyes of his could seduce the pants off a girl without him even trying. Not to mention the little cleft in his chin.

"Are you a virgin?"

That got her eyes open. "Would that shock you?"

"Yes."

"Well, don't worry. I'm not."

"Okay, then." He rinsed the washcloth and went over her face with it once more.

"Kate told me all about you," she said, bliss taking over her body. "She said you surprised her."

"Oh? How?"

"She figured you were an out-and-out hound dog, but then you turned out to be a gentleman."

He grunted.

"No, really. She said you made no pretense about not wanting anything serious, but you weren't only thinking of yourself. She liked you."

"She dumped me."

"Doesn't matter. She thought you were hot."

"Hot, huh?"

His hand went behind her back and she let him push

her forward. He washed her back, then rinsed it, and she just sat there like a lump.

"You want your hair washed?"

She nodded.

"You got it. Now, lean back and close your eyes."

He dipped her into the warmth, holding her steady. She thought of movies she'd seen of people being baptized. The congregants had worn white robes, but still, it was just like that, and not only because of how he held her. She had lost the last of her innocence tonight. She'd taken a life, had seen her world turn to ashes.

He lifted her back up, and then he did the most amazing thing in the whole world. He poured shampoo in his hands and he washed her hair. So gently, so wonderfully, it was miraculous, life-changing, and he just kept massaging and massaging.

"You like that?"

She made some kind of sound, something in the affirmative vein.

He chuckled and he didn't stop.

She jerked again, and blinked. She must have fallen asleep.

"Let's get you rinsed off and put you to bed," he said.

"Okay," she mumbled.

She struggled to stay awake while he rinsed the shampoo out of her hair. Then he stood her up and got her out of the tub. Instantly, there was a big fluffy towel around her, and he dried her with the same care.

He led her out of the bath and when they were next to the bed he drew back the covers.

She looked at him. "I don't have pajamas."

"It's okay."

"You don't either."

"That's okay, too. I'm going to be right over there." He nodded toward a chair by the window.

"No," she said. "You're sleeping with me."

"Tam—"

She turned to him, took hold of his shirt and met his gaze. "Please?"

He didn't answer for a second as he searched her eyes. She felt sure he was going to tell her not to be ridiculous, but then he smiled and said, "Sure."

"Nate?"

"Yeah?"

"Thank you for saving me."

"You saved yourself."

Tam shook her head. "No. You've saved me every single day since I met you."

He leaned down and kissed her on the cheek. "Not yet," he whispered, "but I will. I promise."

That was good enough for her. She climbed into bed, and fell asleep.

BY THE SECOND HOUR OF the weekly status meeting, CEO Leland Ingram felt a trickle of sweat snake down his neck as he forced a laugh. Senator Jackson Raines had told a joke, a bad one, but there wasn't a man in the room who didn't act as if Raines was as funny as Leno.

Ingram admired the senator but he didn't like the son of a bitch one damn bit. Still, there was no option but for Leland to smile, say the right thing at the right time and do some major ass kissing. That's just the way it went, and Leland was nothing if not a pragmatic. He might be officially in charge of Omicron's day-to-day business, but Raines was the guiding force behind its highly secret operation. One that benefited them both.

Raines sat in the king's chair in the conference room. It was slightly higher, slightly bigger and at the head of the table so everyone else in the meeting would have to look up at him. The decorator who'd done this building and Omicron's office in Colorado hadn't understood the necessity of the king's chair until Leland had explained it to him. Men need to know who's boss, who has the final say. In this pansy-ass age of political correctness, it wasn't words that communicated, it was body language, position, the king's seat.

Raines brought in the money. Therefore, he was the king pin. He'd called the meeting for 7:00 a.m., knowing it would be difficult for the managers to get here so early. When Leland's secretary had proposed bringing in coffee and Danish, Raines had given an emphatic no. It was all games. Games with damned high stakes.

Leland himself was the Prince Regent and soon the dynamic was going to shift in his favor. Not today. Today there were going to be fireworks. Nonetheless when the shipment went out and Leland put the money in Omicron's secret offshore account, Raines would have to give Leland his due.

"Thank you, gentlemen," the senator said, leaning back in his chair.

That's all that needed to be said. The underlings

moved out in an orderly fashion, taking BlackBerrys and PDAs with them, leaving Ingram to hear the private word.

When the door to the conference room closed, Leland prepared by focusing his gaze on the bridge of Raines's nose. It would appear, from the king's seat, as if his eyes were slightly downcast, but not subservient. That he might be receiving a dressing-down, but he wasn't a toady.

"We didn't get the chemist," Raines said, his voice muted. "We didn't get her data. And we lost three men."

"We found her once, we'll find her again. We know she's still in L.A. And we destroyed the lab."

"You found her and lost her. She could be anywhere by now. And the lab was never the problem."

"We're on it."

"You're on it?"

That was about fifteen decibels louder. By the end of the conversation, Leland fully expected to hear him roar with rage.

"What the fuck does that mean, you're on it? Do you know where she is at this moment? Do you know if she's still connected to that Delta Force bunch? Where's the soldier who escaped from Colorado? What the hell kind of operation is this, that you can't find a few grunts and a chemist?"

There it was. The roar. The voice that carried across the senate floor. Now Leland's gaze moved down a half inch and he let his shoulders sag by the same degree. "Senator, I've replaced the man in charge and I believe the new man will have the Delta team within the week."

"Based on what, exactly?"

"We're meeting later to go over the details. I'll give you an update first thing tomorrow."

"I'd better have answers I can count on, Leland. We cannot have this situation exposed. The American people have a great need for the money we're bringing in with this weapon. A great need, indeed. I will not disappoint the American people, are we clear?"

"Yes, Senator. Completely."

"I want that update by seven."

"Yes, sir."

Raines leaned back and his posture eased. "Bring me up to speed on the plant."

This was the part of the meeting Leland had been waiting for. He had no idea how in hell they were going to find the scientist or the soldiers. Eventually, they'd make a mistake and that would be that. Of course, he couldn't say that to Raines, but he wasn't too worried. Not yet.

Now, the plant, on the other hand, had exceeded his expectations. Putting it inside the Air Force base had been a stroke of genius, particularly as even the road leading to the perimeter fence was restricted.

Leland felt the same obligation to the citizens of this country as Raines. He wasn't about to let the godless liberals and pantywaists put his country at risk. This country, his country, would not be subject to terrorism again. Not while he still breathed.

# 3

TAMARA'S GASP WOKE NATE from the first sleep he'd had in twenty-two hours, but he was instantly alert. He turned on the bedside lamp to find her eyes were wide open, her mouth, too, and she looked as panicked as a person could be and live through it.

He grabbed her by the shoulders and raised her to a sitting position. When she still didn't look at him, he shook her gently, then not so gently. Finally, she focused, recognized him. Fell completely apart.

It killed him to hear her sobs. In all the time he'd known her, in all the horrendous situations she'd been in, she'd never wept, not like this. It was as if he were listening to a heart shatter, to a world come apart at the seams. Which, of course, it was.

She'd worked so goddamn hard on the dispersal system for the antidote to the gas. When it hadn't worked, something had broken inside her. Although he'd tried to get her to talk about it, she wouldn't. All he knew for sure was that she blamed herself for the failure. Shit, it would have been a miracle if it had worked.

He took her into his arms and comforted her the only way he knew how. He wasn't accustomed to this role, well, not unless he was trying to get laid. Then he had no trouble offering up a shoulder to cry on. This was different.

As far as he was concerned, she was a soldier under his command. He didn't take the responsibility lightly. He'd have given anything to have kept her safe. If there was anyone in the room who'd failed, it was him. He hadn't been at the lab to protect her. His precautions weren't sufficient. "How did they know?"

She pushed away from his shoulder to look at him through tear-filled eyes. "What?"

"Nothing. It's not important."

She wiped her cheeks with the back of her hand, then sniffed again. "I had a bad dream."

"I could tell," he said, wanting to touch her, but painfully aware that she was naked and that the comforter had fallen to her waist. "Want to talk about it?"

"Not really," she said, "but I probably should." She gazed around the room, stopping at the window. He'd made sure the blackout curtains were closed, knowing how badly she needed to sleep. "What time is it?"

He looked at his watch. "Almost eleven."

"In the morning, right?"

"Yeah."

When she was settled, she pulled the comforter up, covering her breasts. He dragged his gaze up to her face. He tended to think of her as delicate because she was so petite. Though her long hair was black and straight and her eyes were darkly Asian, her skin was creamy pale, as if she'd never been in the sun. But he knew she was tough, stronger than she even realized.

"I heard someone coming down the stairs, but you hadn't called. So I got the gun and the flash drive and I hid, you know, in that fake closet."

The previous tenants had thought of everything, including false walls and trick doors.

"They searched the place for a long time. I heard them breaking things and cursing. I just stayed as quiet as I could."

The words were so easily spoken, but he could just imagine how terrified she must have been. He should have been there. "When did you call me?"

She looked at him quizzically. "I didn't have the phone. I was so busy thinking about the data, I forgot it."

"But I got a call. From your cell."

"Who was it?"

"That was just it. No one spoke. I answered, then I heard a gunshot."

"There was a fire. I couldn't stay hidden or I would have burned to death and taken the data with me. When I pushed out the wall, the man was standing right in front of me. I shot him."

He liked to think of her as his soldier, but the truth was, she wasn't. Before they'd met, she'd never even held a gun.

"You know," she said, pushing her hair behind her shoulder. "I think that's why I was able to kill him."

"What was?"

"He hesitated. Because he was dialing the cell phone. He didn't get his gun up quickly enough."

"Let's hear it for the phone company," Nate said sardonically.

"After that, I ran. I headed straight for the stairs. I know someone was behind me, but it was so dark out there I wasn't as afraid of him as I was of falling down an elevator shaft. I went straight to plan B, but I was sure he was going to catch me. I could practically feel the bullet in my back."

He knew exactly what she was talking about. If anyone ever did invent eyes in the back of the head, he'd be first in line with the check. "You lost him."

She nodded. "I don't know how."

"Training. That's what it's all about. I'm just sorry I wasn't there sooner."

"How could you have known?"

"The question is, how did they know? I would have expected them to find me long before you. That lab was way the hell off the radar."

"I don't know. I also don't know what they took out before they torched the place."

"Every computer in there was wired to blow without the proper access keys," Nate assured her. "They won't get anything important."

"But they'll know that I was working, and they'd have to be stupid not to realize I was all over the antidote."

"Yeah, that's probably true."

"Which means…"

"That whatever they're planning, the timetable just moved up."

"Oh, crap," she said, with such a heavy sigh that it made Nate laugh.

"I don't think it's very funny."

"It's not. It's a damn tragedy. But all we can do is what we can do."

She shook her head, looking at him seriously, as if she *needed* him to hear her. He lost his smile and listened.

"I don't want to die alone," she said.

He almost spoke, but the words had been uttered so softly, so *forcefully,* that he waited and thought. With her hair a wild dark tangle, her eyes puffy from crying and her skin so smooth all he wanted was to touch her, he understood clearly. It wasn't that she was almost killed last night, or that she'd had to take a life, but that she was alone. Had been alone for months. He had Seth, Boone, Cade. They all understood exactly what it was to be a soldier. They knew what the risks were, how to cope with the unbearable stress of a mission that seemed to have no end. Even Kate and Christie were holding up their end. But Tam had been forced into a bubble, a tiny world where there was no one to lean on or to question or run her ideas by. She'd been flying solo since Kosovo, and she was exhausted.

He nodded slowly, wondering briefly how he could justify kidnapping another biochemist to work with her. That was no answer. He had none. "What can I do?"

"I'm not sure," she said. "But you can start by taking off your clothes."

"Pardon me?"

Her cheeks had blushed a vivid pink and her hands were twisted tightly together but she looked him right in the eyes. "I think, I hope, that I haven't been wildly off the mark with you being attracted to me."

He thought she was going to continue but when she just kept staring, he nodded. "Yeah." It was an understatement, but he wasn't exactly at his best at the moment.

"I'm attracted to you, too. And since the odds of us living long, happy lives is about one in a million, I think we should do whatever we can in whatever time we have that brings us pleasure. And happiness. And comfort."

He ought to have some kind of reasonable argument. He was the team leader. He was responsible for her, for all of them. Having sex would complicate things in ways he couldn't possibly foresee. But all he kept thinking was *thank you, God. Thank you, thank you.*

"On the other hand, if I'm totally freaking you out, we can pretend I never said a word."

"What?"

She looked away, then back again. "Nate, cut it out. If you don't want to, just say so."

"Don't want to? Oh, Tam…"

"Oh, Tam, what?" She looked down pointedly. "Naked here. Can we say vulnerable?"

"Vulnera— Shit. I'm sorry. No. I want to. I just haven't thought about us actually, you know…"

"You haven't *thought* about it? Wow. I have. A lot."

"You have?"

She nodded. "I had a lot of time alone in that lab."

"That's great," he said. "Seriously, that's great, because I have, too."

"But you just said—"

"Don't listen to me. I think I had a small stroke when you asked me to take off my clothes. I'm better now."

Her smile blossomed and it made everything in the world feel as soft and clean as the pretty white sheets. "You're weird, but then I've always liked weird."

"Thanks."

She laughed. "So we're just gonna talk about it?"

"Huh?"

Her eyes rolled, but she didn't lose the grin. "I meant now."

"Oh. Oh!"

She flopped her hands on the comforter as she shook her head. "How long has it been for you?"

His shirt was already on the floor, and he was in the middle of toeing off his socks and undoing his belt. "Doesn't matter."

"No?"

He shook his head as he unzipped his fly. "Nope. None of it mattered until right this minute."

"Because…"

He slipped off his jeans and his boxers then jumped under the covers. He found her hand and squeezed it gently. "Because now it's you."

KATE AND VINCE HAD COME to Boone and Christie's room at one-thirty. The new arrivals had already checked into the motel, using other names of course, and Seth and Boone had helped them put in the security devices on the front door, the windows and the telephone. Christie and Harper were working at their waitressing jobs. Cade was due in an hour via Greyhound. None of them had heard a word from Nate or Tam.

"All he said was that she'd been compromised," Kate

related. She sat on the ugly beige couch that was the twin to the one in her room. Vince was next to her, close, touching from shoulder to knee. Milo, Christie's golden lab, had curled up near her feet.

Seth stood in the kitchen making a fresh pot of coffee and Boone sat by the small round table in the corner. Both men looked as if they hadn't slept in a while, and she wondered what these nighttime missions were costing them.

"Christie said he sounded tense." Boone bent forward, leaning his elbows on his thighs. "She didn't think Tam was taken, but maybe she was hurt."

"That might explain why we haven't heard anything."

"Maybe."

Seth came back into the room. He seemed a lot more comfortable with his prosthetic claw, and Kate figured doing his job again had made the difference. Truth be known, she still felt guilty that he'd lost his hand fighting to save her life. It didn't seem to matter that it was Omicron bullets that had blown his hand almost all the way off. The guilt was hers and his new ease with his prosthesis didn't take it away. At least he had Harper now. Kate hadn't seen them for a couple of weeks, but she'd heard they were doing great.

"I don't like it," Vince said. "If we don't hear soon, we're going to have to make some decisions."

"Like what?" Kate asked.

"Like what to do if they don't come back."

Kate shook her head. "They'll be here. Nate wouldn't let them get her, not Tam." She turned to Boone and Seth. "What do you guys need us to do?"

Seth smiled. "Robbing a bank would be most helpful."

Vince laughed. "I could probably pull it off, but man, don't let 'em send me to an L.A. court." Vince had been a detective in L.A. for over ten years.

"Seriously," Boone said. "What we need most now is cash. Christie and Harper are working double shifts at that damn truck stop, but the tips aren't that great."

"I suppose," Vince asked, "that Harper can't let anyone know she's a doctor."

"Nope. Too chancy. We're stuck paying for these rooms." Seth got up again and poured himself a cup of coffee. He looked around questioningly, but no one else wanted any. "We thought about renting a house, but we haven't found anywhere we could all stay that's discreet enough. We're too damn close to the Omicron plant to take any risks."

"We'll find jobs," Kate assured him.

"No, wait," Vince said, turning to look at her. "We've got some cash. I think we should put all our energy on breaking Omicron's back. Waiting tables isn't going to bring in enough to make a difference anyway."

"Are you sure?" Kate asked.

"I'm sure."

Seth frowned. "What are we talking about here? A couple thousand…"

"Over a hundred thousand," Vince said. "And I can get it here without it being traced or reported to the government."

Seth's brows lifted in surprise. "Good man."

"Selfish man." Vince nodded at Kate. "I want her safe. That's all that matters."

Kate squeezed his hand, but caught Boone looking suspiciously hungry.

"So how long until the money can be here?" Boone asked.

"Already?" Kate was teasing. She knew exactly how desperate the money situation was. Besides, she was so busy being proud of Vince she could barely hide her grin. Man, was he ever going to get lucky tonight.

"There's a room in the plant that has a biometric scanner to gain entry," Boone said. "We're pretty sure it's where the gas is either stored or poured. Either way, we need access."

"You mean it reads fingerprints?" she asked.

Seth nodded.

"How are you going to get past that? Aside from borrowing someone's hand?"

Boone smiled. "Well, now that you mention it, Katie, that's exactly what we intend to do. But, we'll need some cash to pull it off."

TAM LET THE COMFORTER fall once more to her waist as she moved closer to Nate. It took her a minute to get her breathing under control after that last statement. It hadn't even been the lovely words. It was how deeply he'd meant them.

She'd known for a long time that he wanted her, but she thought it was because she was simply there. Because he had so few options. Her mind couldn't quite grasp that she'd been so very, very wrong.

"What's the matter?" he asked. He scooted closer to her, and she felt his naked skin brush against hers.

"I'm not very good at this kind of thing."

"Don't worry about it. You're perfect."

"We haven't done anything yet."

He smiled. "Trust me. You're perfect."

She knew it was a line, but what the hell. She'd told him the truth about why she wanted this. She needed to be close to someone, to feel alive again. But she hadn't told him everything.

He leaned in and she knew this was it. If he kissed her, it would change things forever. She still had a moment to call things off.

She parted her lips and closed her eyes.

His mouth brushed against hers. Soft lips, warm breath, slightly cautious. He didn't press, just skimmed lightly, letting her get comfortable, she supposed.

It wasn't what she wanted, however well intentioned. There was only one thing to do about that. She put her hand behind his neck, held him steady, and kissed him. Hard. Exactly the way she'd fantasized for all those months.

He got with the program right quick. His tongue slipped past her teeth, and he took over. That was fine with her. She moved her hand down his back then across his shoulders, amazed at the feel of him. She'd never been with a soldier before, or anyone who looked remotely like they could have been one. Nate's body was like something out of a movie or a magazine. Wide shoulders, perfectly sculpted abs, slim waist and hips, long legs.

God, she had to stop thinking about it or she'd be too self-conscious to do another thing.

Besides, it was much more fun to enjoy the wonderful things he was doing to her mouth. She'd always loved kissing, but in theory, not in practice. With Nate, she was in the advanced course, and it was immediately clear that he had a lot to teach her.

Take the way he nipped her lower lip. It hurt, but not in a bad way. Then there was his tongue which got hard and pointy, then soft, then hard again. He explored her carefully and gave her the courage to explore right back.

The moment she ventured out with her own tongue, he sucked it into his mouth. It sent shivers down her body, and she could only deduce that if he was this good at kissing, he'd be freakin' amazing at everything else.

He pulled back, and she was about to complain, but then he kicked off the covers so she was able to see him all over. That chest. It was stunning. Just enough dark hair to make him manly, not carpeted. Her gaze moved down, and oh—

He moved a hand to her shoulder to ease her down, but she batted it away. She'd seen penises before. But this was a whole new ball game. So to speak.

"What's wrong?"

"I'm impressed."

He looked down. "That old thing? I've had it for years."

She laughed, but she didn't look away.

"Come on, Tam. It's not that big a deal."

"Yes, it is. It's just so, well, hard."

He laughed this time. "Who the hell have you been with?"

"Clearly the wrong men."

He didn't just laugh this time. His head went back and he laughed so loud she was sure the people in the next room heard.

"I'm not joking."

He sighed out loud as he pulled her in for another kiss. When he pulled back, he met her gaze with smiling eyes. "I know. I know, and you're amazing, so look where you want, touch what you feel like and don't mind me. I'll love it all."

"Really?"

He nodded.

She grinned as she scooted down the bed. When she looked up at him again, the laughter had left his eyes. But he didn't stop her.

# 4

_____

NATE WASN'T SURE WHAT he was supposed to do. This wasn't going according to any of his usual scripts. Most of the time, he took the lead. He was a big, tough soldier after all, and the ladies really seemed to like that. From time to time the lady in question would want to show him her colors, which was also fine by him. This experience was something completely different.

Tam had crawled under the covers and moved things around so that the comforter draped him from the waist down. All he could see of her was an undulating lump moving toward his groin. Maybe he should have been a bit more specific about the whole touching thing.

He had to fight the urge to throw back the covers, or at the very least move. She'd looked happy. Excited. More importantly, distracted.

He knew this was a risky venture. One he probably should have nipped in the bud. There was no way he could justify his actions as purely selfless. But he wasn't being a total bastard, either.

Tam was right. If they'd found her once, they could find her again. The odds of survival shrunk daily, and even if they did make it, running from Omicron was as stressful as any wartime scenario. She didn't want to be alone. He didn't, either. Even if all the sex did was offer a distraction, that was enough. In fact, it was— "Shit."

She'd taken his cock in hand, and she hadn't been a delicate flower about it. "Hey, take it easy down there."

He heard a muffled giggle, then she moved her hand up his shaft.

His eyes closed at the sensation of someone else's hand rubbing him. It had been a long time. Too long. More than that, it was Tamara's hand, and he'd had too many dreams about this to be a hundred percent sure he wouldn't wake up any second.

Her soft palm moved down again, then all the way up to the incredibly sensitive glans. There was no choice but to move. It felt so amazingly good he was worried that things might end prematurely. "Tam?"

She didn't answer. She just kept rubbing. When her other hand cupped his balls, he nearly jumped off the bed. He threw back the covers and she looked at him with brown eyes filled with mischief. Not terror, not sadness. "Is something wrong?" she asked.

"No. I just wanted to see you."

"Okay," she said. "I was gonna come out in a second anyway."

"Curiosity sated?"

"Not even close." She let him go and slithered up the sheet until her head was on her pillow. "I've been looking in test tubes for too long. Humans seem so fascinating."

He shifted until he was on his side, head on his hand, his eyes about level with hers. "Humans, huh?"

She nodded. "In particular, human male soldiers

who have dark brown hair and green eyes, and have sneaky little clefts in their chins."

"Lucky me, I seem to fit the criteria."

She nodded again as she searched his face. "Do me a favor?"

"Anything."

"If this is a pity screw, don't tell me. I don't want to know."

"Pity? What are you, high?"

"Good answer."

"Not a line."

"I know," she said. "Now you need to give me another good answer."

"What's the question?"

"Do you have a condom?"

"As a matter of fact, I do."

"I think it's time to get it."

He leaned over and kissed her soft, plush lips, then turned over to fetch his jeans from the floor. In his back pocket there was a smaller pocket, and in that were two condoms. He left one because they couldn't stay here indefinitely no matter how much he wanted to.

When he turned back to Tam, she was nibbling on her lower lip, something he'd seen her do in the lab when faced with a problem. "What's wrong?"

"Nothing."

"You know we can stop this right here," he said.

"I don't want to stop."

"But you're worried."

"I just think too much." She put her arms over her head and closed her eyes. "Make me stop. Please."

He couldn't do anything but stare at her. When he'd first met her in Kosovo, he hadn't thought that much about her. He hadn't thought of her as a great beauty, although he'd found her attractive, and she hadn't been a particularly memorable conversationalist. He'd been shocked when he found out she was a biochemist, and a brilliant one.

As he'd come to know her over the last year, she'd become more and more beautiful to him, so much so that there were times he'd had to turn away. Maybe it was her mixed Asian-American heritage that made her loveliness so subtle, but he doubted it. Back in Kosovo, he just hadn't been paying attention.

There had been nights when the thought of her face alone had kept him going. When he looked at her now, so trusting, he wanted her so badly he trembled.

"Nate?"

Her eyes had opened and she looked at him expectantly. He still held the condom in his hand. "One sec." He brought the small packet to his teeth and ripped it open. Oddly, he felt a little embarrassed putting it on. Maybe because he was so goddamned turned on he was afraid he'd blow it any second.

He kept it together long enough to make it safe. Long enough to pull Tam into his arms and kiss her. It wasn't going to be one of those record-breaking marathons. And he sure as hell wasn't going to last until she came. So he needed to make sure she came first.

He touched her face as he kissed her, moving in slow motion. His fingers trailed down her jaw, her neck, the tender skin above her breasts.

He kissed her hard and touched her softly, then squeezed her breast as he brushed her lips with his. It was all sensation and heat and the noises she made at the back of her throat. His world became the way her nipple hardened against his palm, the feel of her ribs.

He floated as he pressed his hand flat on her stomach, as he breathed in her soft gasp. Tiny fireworks went off behind his closed eyes and each sensation made him ache that he'd never again feel it for the first time.

He moaned as she touched the nape of his neck, as her long, slim fingers skimmed his shoulder.

When he slipped his own fingers down past her mound and onto her puffy lips, he drew back, wanting to watch her face as he dipped into her, as he found her clit.

Her mouth opened, her eyelids fluttered and her pale cheeks turned pink. So responsive. She arched her back, her hips moved, her legs parted and the sound she'd held back came out—a low moan that made him want to slay dragons.

He moved his finger faster now, needing her to come a lot more quickly than he should. She had to do it soon, or he would never make it. To miss being inside her was too much to ask. He just wasn't that noble.

Tam pointed her toes as the muscles in her legs tightened. It was the beginning of her climax, and she wasn't sure how she'd gotten there. She was an expert in getting herself off. Living in an underground lab for a year would do that to a person, but this wasn't anything like her solo sessions.

It wasn't just the kissing, but oh, God, the kissing was amazing. She'd thought about Nate's lips a lot, wondering how they would feel, and if he had some magic moves that had made all his conquests fall at his feet. The answer turned out to be yes. And the moves didn't stop with his lips.

How was it possible he was better at this than any other man? He knew exactly how to use his fingers. How much pressure, how fast to move, when to ease up. It was wonderful. Just like she'd imagined only much better.

She gripped his shoulder with one hand, the back of his hair with the other as she prepared to come, her eyes closed tightly, she arched as she slammed into gear.

It was always like that for her—one second anticipation, the next, bam, she was gone. She always had to stop, move her hand away from any sensitive spots, and Nate did that, too. Only he didn't flop on his back and breathe hard, like she was doing. He sat up and grabbed a pillow from the bed. His arm went under her thighs and he lifted her whole bottom half to shove the pillow beneath her butt.

Her eyes had opened during that move, and widened as he settled between her legs. He looked so big staring down at her, and so damn sexy.

Without warning, he thrust himself inside her so hard the whole bed moved. She cried out but not because it hurt or anything. God, no. It was the most amazing feeling in the world. He filled her, lifted her and she would swear that he made her come all over again.

All she could do was go along for the ride. His expression was so intense his teeth had clamped tightly together. She grabbed onto his shoulders, and the muscles she felt made her look. Cords of tendons stood out, his biceps bulged. His nipples were hard and his chest heaved with every thrust. It was all so unreal, and he was so gorgeous, it didn't even feel like her life.

The only guys she'd ever been with had treated her carefully, as if she'd break or something, but not Nate. The gentleness he'd shown her in the tub and with his kisses had gone, leaving only the warrior.

He grunted as he sat up, as he lifted her legs and put one on each shoulder. Then he leaned over her again, bending her almost in two.

She grabbed on to the sheets as he thrust, as he turned her body into a quivering, trembling mess. It was unbelievable, totally outside anything she'd ever felt in her whole life.

He plowed into her one more time, then froze as he came, his neck long and tight, his forehead beaded with sweat, his growl low and long and thrilling.

Finally, he relaxed. He kissed her, but only for a second, then eased back, letting her legs fall to the bed. He pulled out the pillow, and then he fell heavily on his back next to her.

For long minutes, all they did was breathe hard. She gradually became aware of his hip touching hers, of her foot against his calf.

He took her hand in his and squeezed it. "You okay?"

"Oh, yes."

"I didn't hurt you?"

"No. Not even a little."

He sighed. "Good."

She turned to look at him. His chest rose and fell rapidly, his eyes were closed and his hair was wet with sweat. He was the best looking man she'd ever seen.

She had no idea what time it was, or how long they'd been awake. All she knew was that from the moment he'd touched her cheek, she'd forgotten all about last night. The rest of the world and all the horrors it held had disappeared. He'd taken her places she'd never been, and for that, she'd be grateful forever.

She knew it was just sex. She also knew that sometimes just sex was just perfect. "Thank you," she whispered.

He looked at her. "To say it was my pleasure is an incredible understatement."

She grinned and felt stupidly proud. "Cool."

He chuckled and squeezed her hand again.

NATE TOOK A MILITARY shower—get wet, lather up, rinse off, do it again, done in five minutes. He did it alone. Not because he didn't want to shower with Tam. He did. But they had to get out of here, and be quick about it.

As soon as he'd come out of his sex-induced coma, he'd called Seth, who'd given him a choice piece of his mind for worrying them all so much. The whole team had assembled in that crappy, out-of-the-way motel. Nate told him he and Tam would be there in about six hours. Time to get dressed, leave L.A., get something to eat. Then drive the damn speed limit all the way past Vegas.

He missed speeding. He used to do it all the time, before getting pulled over could have deadly consequences. His name was in every database—one call in from a highway cop could end it all. He missed having a private life too, but today had shown him once again that his first responsibility was to the team. To the mission.

Being with Tam had been fucking unbelievable. He wanted nothing more than to be with her again and again. But that wasn't going to happen.

He'd freaked Seth out. They'd all been worried sick that he and Tam had been captured or killed. None of them needed that kind of anxiety, especially not from him.

He dried himself off and put on his clothes, hoping Tam would understand. It wasn't that he regretted his actions, but he should have called Seth and warned him about the delay. The whole episode had confirmed what he'd suspected for months. He liked Tam too much. While he'd been busy distracting her from the nightmare she'd survived, she'd distracted him from his command.

He went back into the main room, where he saw Tam waiting on the bed. She had her clothes on her lap. All the joy had left her face, and she seemed haunted once more.

She needed time, that's all. Time and a purpose. He'd see to that. But first, he'd get her the hell out of Los Angeles. Not that she wouldn't be in danger in Nevada. There would be no real rest until they'd won this fight.

"It's all yours," he said.

"I won't be long."

He nodded, then turned away as she walked naked to the bathroom. It would have been a whole hell of a lot easier if he didn't like her so much. After it was all over, he'd have to see about this. See if what he felt for her was the real deal, or just a matter of circumstance.

For now, he had only one thing he could focus on. Exposing Omicron. Nothing else mattered.

While Tam showered, he passed the time cleaning his gun, and thinking about what came next.

THE SHOWER FELT WONDERFUL, and so did the big fluffy towel as Tam dried off, but putting on her only clothes nearly made her weep.

They smelled of smoke and fear. It was just a T-shirt and jeans, and they would be fine after a wash, but she wanted more than anything to throw them away. She didn't even have clean underwear. She had ditched those, choosing to go commando, and she'd turned her socks inside out, but it all felt wrong.

Was there money to get her new things? Probably not after they paid for the hotel room. Why had he brought her here? This place had to cost at least a hundred a night.

She wiped a clear spot on the mirror, and sighed as she got a load of her hair. She had no brush. No tooth-brush. Nothing except the clothes on her back and a flash drive.

Using her fingers, she tried to make her hair obey, but it was no use. Then she rinsed her mouth out with water, and scrubbed her teeth with her finger, and that was even less successful than her finger comb.

She left the bathroom, and there was Nate standing by the door. He seemed impatient, and she felt the heat rise in her cheeks. She wasn't sure why she was embarrassed. It wasn't because of what they'd done. No, that had been the best thing she'd done in ages. Something else was going on, but she couldn't pinpoint it. Not yet.

"You ready?"

She nodded. "I'd really appreciate it if we could stop at a gas station with a mini-mart. I need a toothbrush and a few other things."

"You got it."

She looked at him again, at his businesslike tone and she had to know. "Are you sorry?"

His shoulders sagged and he walked right up to her. He lifted her chin so he could look her straight in the eyes. "No. Don't ever think that. I haven't felt that wonderful in so long, I can't even tell you. But I should have called the team. They were worried."

"I understand."

He hesitated, then he leaned down and kissed her lightly on the lips. "I'll never forget this."

She smiled, but his words didn't comfort. She would have pressed, but they needed to go. And she needed to think.

What did she want from him? She'd asked him to help her forget, and he'd done just that. She'd figured since it had been so great that they'd do it again. But that was an assumption she needed to examine.

He opened the door and she knew the moment she stepped into the hallway that she had to give up her little fantasy. She wasn't at all sure what would come next, just that what had prompted her to proposition him in the first place was still true. She didn't want to die alone.

Now she had to wonder if she'd meant she needed someone, or if she'd meant she'd needed Nate.

# 5

I⊤ HAD BEEN A BRUTAL SHIFT at the truck stop where it felt to Harper as if every employee and soldier from Nellis had come by not to eat, but to complain. She wasn't used to the relentlessness of being a waitress. As a doctor, she rarely had to do terribly physical labor, and she never had to kiss anyone's ass for a tip. No matter how tempting it was to get angry, she didn't. It simply wouldn't have done any good.

Since the night she'd realized she had to face up to her situation, she'd had revelation after revelation, most of them good. She'd accepted that through no fault of her own she was part of this. She was being hunted by Omicron, and if she didn't do something about it, she would be killed. There was no use pretending she hadn't seen an entire village in Serbia wiped out by the lethal gas. That she didn't know exactly who was responsible for those deaths.

She'd also come to accept that even though it wasn't easy for her, she needed to trust the people around her. Seth was her biggest breakthrough. She'd never believed that someone could love her, that she could love someone in return, but then he'd come into her life. Who would have guessed that while he was healing from having his hand blown off, he'd be the one to heal her heart? She wasn't a sappy person, not by a long shot, but even she couldn't deny that something miraculous had taken place during the worst of situations.

Going to work each day at the truck stop wasn't that bad. The money was ludicrously low, but it helped. It was a damn shame, however, that she couldn't use her medical degree. They could have all used the money.

Christie, who'd gotten her the job, had been anxious all afternoon. Boone had called her, filling her in about Nate and Tam not showing up. But, like Harper, Christie couldn't afford to miss even an hour of work, so she'd soldiered on. Harper had tried to tell her that her brother was fine, that he was too smart to get caught, but Christie wouldn't be satisfied until she saw Nate.

It would have been great if they'd walked into Christie's room at the motel and found that Nate and Tam had arrived, but no. It was still good to see Kate and Vince. And here was Cade, whom she'd heard about but never met.

He was quite large. Conan large. But he had a shy smile and his sandy brown hair had a cowlick in the back, reminiscent of Dennis the Menace. She wondered if the guys in his unit had given him hell for it, but then he'd probably had a crew cut back then.

"I'm Harper," she said, extending her hand.

He shook it almost too gently, as if he knew he could easily hurt her. "Ma'am."

"How was your trip?"

He shrugged. "Okay, I suppose. It was tricky getting the boxes on board. Security is tighter now, even at the bus stations."

"Boxes?"

"Weapons," he said. "We've collected quite a few, and we couldn't afford to leave them behind."

"Of course," she said. She'd been told he was a sniper. An excellent one. She shivered, still not used to the nearness of death.

Even being together in one room like this was incredibly dangerous. But, then so was everything else. They would either come up with a way to defeat Omicron, or they wouldn't. Right now all she could do was spend as much time as possible with Seth.

"Nate and Tam are on their way," Boone said. "He called."

Harper hadn't even realized how on edge she'd been about them until her shoulders relaxed.

"Thank God," Christie said. "Let me get something to drink, then catch us up, okay?"

Harper went with her, wishing she could have showered before this meeting.

"Actually," Boone continued, "there's good news for you and Harper. Vince here has generously decided to bankroll us, at least for now. So you two won't have to go back to that truck stop."

Harper looked at Christie and they both grinned like idiots. "Gee, what a shame," Harper said. "I'll so miss coming home smelling like burgers and onion rings."

"I'm assuming we won't be laying about eating bonbons," Christie added.

Boone shook his head. "I wish you could, but no. There's work to be done."

Harper poured herself a cold soda and Christie went for iced tea. Boone didn't wait until they returned. He filled them in on their discovery of the chamber, and the biometric hand scanner that stood in their way.

When she joined the others, she sat on the floor next to Seth. He looked exhausted, but that was nothing new.

"We need to get into that chamber," Boone said. "We're pretty sure we have a way, but it hinges on a kidnapping."

Harper smiled. "Well, as long as it's not anything illegal."

Boone grinned back. "That's not all. The subject can't know he was kidnapped. And we're going to need him for at least three hours. Can it be done?"

She thought a moment, then nodded. "There are a couple of drugs that we could use. Rohypnol could work, but there's even less chance of him remembering with gamma-hydroxybutyrate. GHB is odorless, colorless, tasteless and given the proper dose, it should knock out the subject for several hours. Might be hard to give you just three, though. More like five to eight."

Boone looked at Seth. "That could work, right?"

"Yeah. Especially if we find the right man leaving the Renegade."

Harper hadn't been to the Renegade, but she'd seen the bar every day on her way to work. It was a local hangout, and a lot of people from the base went there. They had pool tables and video poker and lots of cold beer.

Seth squeezed her arm, then turned to Vince. "You're sure you can get us the Mikrosil?"

Vince nodded. "I'll have it in a couple of days."

"What's Mikrosil?" Christie asked. "And why are we kidnapping someone?"

"We have to get past the scanner," Seth explained. "The only way to do that is to use the fingerprints of someone with access. We're going to make a glove out of Mikrosil, using our subject's hand. We slip on the glove, which has all his fingerprints intact, and voilà. We're in."

"Hey," Cade said. He was standing by the window, peering out between the yellowed blinds. "It's Nate."

ELI SAT IN THE MIDDLE of rush hour traffic in his ancient Toyota Camry, praying the car wouldn't die. It had once been something to be proud of, but that had been fifteen years ago, and the man who'd been proud was his father. Eli had inherited the four-door sedan in high school. Until recently, he'd figured he'd drive it to death, then get another used car to take its place.

It had been a good, if frugal, decision—one his parents were pleased with. Eli had been taught from infancy to save, to be prepared, to have a something socked away for a rainy day. It was in his nature now, and something he'd given little thought to. Until he'd walked into Corky Baker's house and found the veteran reporter dead. Until, in a moment of sheer insanity, he'd volunteered to continue Baker's exposé of Omicron. Not to mention the late night phone call warning him that he should sleep with his gun under his pillow.

He inched along the freeway, glancing at his temperature gauge first, then the rearview mirror. As if he'd know if someone was following him. Right. The guy in the Explorer behind him could be an Omicron operative whose sole objective was to take him out.

One thing had become clear since that phone call from Nate. Eli had found his rainy day. If he was going to die, and soon, what did he want to do with his last days? Drive this car? Live in his tiny, ugly apartment? Devote every moment to work, or try to sow whatever wild oats he could when he wasn't directly risking his life?

Not that he wouldn't continue digging up dirt on Omicron. His focus at the moment was on Senator Jackson Raines. There was a seemingly impenetrable aura of secrecy surrounding Raines. So far Eli hadn't found a single person who was willing to say anything about Raines, even off the record. Eli wished his connections were better, but using Baker's name was at least gaining him some access. He'd just have to be more persistent, that's all. And a hell of a lot cagier.

As for the rest of it?

He took the next available off-ramp, which happened to be Ventura Boulevard. He knew just where he wanted to go from here, and the closer he got to his destination, the more his decision made sense.

He could thank his folks for this, and he would, in a letter they'd receive upon his death. He shivered at the image of his mother weeping, and thought instead about how much he had in his savings account, his CDs, his money market fund. It was a lot. Especially for someone twenty-three.

Mostly, the money had been left to him by his grandparents, and it had been earmarked for his retirement.

If he used it, there would be hefty penalties. But since the odds of him actually retiring were damn slim, and, wait—there it was.

He pulled into the first space reserved for clients. Said a quiet goodbye to the trusty Camry, then headed inside. As soon as he walked in the door, he saw it.

A brand-new, just off the assembly line, bright red 911 Turbo Porsche with all-wheel drive, 3.6 liter engine, six cylinders, rain sensors, leather seats, an on-board computer, Bose Surround Sound, PCM with color display, thirteen speakers and a six disc CD auto changer. *Oh, yeah.*

As he ran his hand over the gleaming top he got a little hard. He'd get nothing from the trade-in, of course, but he'd give them a nice deposit. Maybe ten thousand against one hundred and twenty. With his credit, he'd have no problem. He tried to feel guilty about not being around to pay off the car, but hey, they could repossess it when he croaked.

Two salesmen were coming at him from either side of the showroom. He smiled, waiting to see who would win. Actually, he already knew. Sensible Eli was driving out of here in his very impractical dream car. Tomorrow, he'd find himself a decent place to live. Hell, he might even call Janice Tucker, the girl he'd been in love with since high school. He pictured her expression when he drove up in this stunner.

TAM'S STOMACH WAS IN KNOTS as she got out of the vehicle at the motel. She wasn't surprised they were staying at such a dive, but it seemed hard to believe the place was still in business. Everything about it was filthy, broken or both.

There weren't many cars back here, and the parking lot wasn't visible from the road. Hell, most of the road to this place was hidden by a rotting fence, some scraggly trees and a liquor store.

This was Nevada, though, so she supposed there would be places like this wherever there was gambling. She wondered if there were any other tenants, or if the team alone was keeping the owner solvent for yet another month.

"Everything okay?"

She smiled at Nate, trying to reassure herself more than him. "Sure. Let's go."

He held her arm as they walked across the cracked pavement. She'd slept almost all the way from L.A. He'd gotten her a toothbrush and paste, a hairbrush, a sample-size deodorant and they'd eaten a couple of fast food burgers. The next thing she knew he was shaking her awake.

She hadn't met several of the team yet. Christie, for one. Vince. She knew the Delta guys from Kosovo. Harper and Kate, too. But she barely remembered Cade or Boone. And now she'd be living amongst them.

It should have made her happy being in the real—if often terrifying—aboveground world. In truth it unnerved her. She'd been alone for so long.

Nate didn't have to knock. The door swung open and they were ushered inside. Nate got the big hellos, starting with a crushing hug from his sister. They all seemed relieved that he'd arrived. She understood that.

Harper and Kate approached her shyly, but gave her hugs nonetheless, which was nice. Clearly they all knew about the lab.

"Coffee?" Christie asked. "Food?"

"Both would be great," Nate said. "And we need to put together some clothes for Tam. Is there somewhere inexpensive that has the basics?"

Christie nodded. "There's a Goodwill store in town. We'll take her, but first, what the hell happened?"

Nate looked at the small couch, then the chairs by the round table. Kate got up and sat down in front of Vince, leaving room for two on the couch. They sat down while Christie and Boone went to the kitchen.

Tam felt Nate's concern for her. Sideways glances, brief touches on the back or arm. He wanted her to be okay, to feel included, but that was not possible, at least not yet.

Maybe if she hadn't been wearing her singed, dirty clothes. Or if she'd had a chance to put on a little makeup. This whole group thing was going to take some time, that's all. For now, she'd let Nate tell whatever story he cared to. She doubted he would include the part where they'd had sex.

Just thinking about it made her blush, and she wished there weren't so many of them in the cramped space. She wasn't sure where she was going to sleep, or what she was going to do with herself now that she wasn't working on the antidote. Would they expect her to get a job? She'd never worked outside of a school or a lab. Never. She hadn't been a waitress or a babysitter or anything normal. Her parents had insisted that she concentrate on academics. Her mother taught high school mathematics and her father was a physics professor at Berkeley. She'd tried so hard to make them proud. God, she'd screwed that up. And now, here was yet another avenue where she could fail.

She closed her eyes, willing herself not to go down that path. There was too much at stake to dwell in depression. A job that challenged her in new ways might do her some good.

"Tam?"

She looked up. Kate had a sandwich on a paper plate in one hand, and a cup of coffee in the other.

"Thank you," she said, taking the food and drink.

"Nate said you liked fake sugar and skim milk?"

Tam looked at him, already eating his sandwich. "Yes, thanks."

"Just so you know, everyone gets one freebie. After this, if you're hungry, you get to make it yourself."

It wasn't a reprimand, not when the accompanying smile was so friendly. So she smiled back.

While they ate, Nate told them details about the men at the lab and what had taken place after she'd escaped. He related it between swallows, and made the whole hotel thing seem vague and unimportant.

Then Seth took over, explaining what they'd seen at the plant, and their solution to getting past the security. She listened, but mostly she watched the others. She would have to work with these people, trust them with her life.

The one thing that was completely consistent was their respect for Nate. No one interrupted him. They asked questions, but if he sidestepped a firm answer, they didn't press. It was as if they were his children, his followers, which, she supposed, they were.

She'd seen him in battle when he'd saved her from certain death in Kosovo. His strength had been undeniable. She'd felt it here, too, although he was always kind and funny when he came to see her. And he'd always come through. With food, clothing, lab equipment, even a whole cloud chamber for her experiments. No wonder everyone listened so intently. Nate got it done. No excuses, no second best. He just did the job, and that was that. He'd never mention it again, either. It was easy to expect him to succeed with everything.

She sat back on the couch. How could she have been so obtuse? Nate had more pressure on him than any of them. He was the leader, and everyone, she saw now, simply expected him to lead them to victory. Damn. Her failure at the lab put the ball right back in Nate's court. No one expected him to come up with a dispersal system, but they fully expected him to come up with a way around it.

Hers had been one task in a big picture. Nate had the whole deal to handle. Taking care of her needs was so far down on the list it was laughable.

It hurt to even think it, but she couldn't ask him again. If she needed someone to keep her sane, she'd have to look elsewhere. She wouldn't be able to live with herself if she caused him to fail.

Crap. Everyone was looking at her, and she hadn't heard a word.

"I have a job for her," Nate said. "In fact, I've got

jobs for all of you." He looked at his sister. "But let's get Tam squared away on the clothes while we can, okay? We've got a long night ahead of us."

He stood up and got his wallet out. He handed Tam almost a hundred dollars. "Get what you need."

She would never spend it all. She'd learned how to do without. Not a bad skill for someone on the run.

The others had stood, waiting for Nate's directive. She was curious about this job he had for her, but he had turned to Boone. "I need you guys here tonight. I'm going to need all your opinions and arguments. It's going to be damn tricky to pull this off, and I won't be satisfied until we've covered every possible outcome."

"Pull this off?" Seth asked. "Are you talking about the whole enchilada here? Exposing Omicron and the men behind it?"

Nate took in a deep breath. "If it all works, then yes. If it doesn't…"

"We're screwed. But hey, we're screwed anyway, right?" Seth pulled Harper close with his good hand. "We might as well go out with a bang."

Tam watched Nate's reaction, seeing the weight of his responsibility in his face. There were lines around his mouth, his eyes. She knew he was in his early thirties, but he seemed much older.

"You ready?" Christie asked, touching her arm.

She wanted to put off the clothes thing, to just sit down and hear Nate's plan. But she nodded. "Sure."

Nate didn't touch her but got her attention nonetheless. "I'm going to get us a room," he said. "I'll be here when you get back."

Tam followed Christie out to her old truck, wondering if Nate had meant what she thought he meant. A room for the two of them? With one bed? Her first reaction was relief. Being with him made her feel safer than she had in years. And the sex—it had been life-changing. She used to think it wasn't worth all the ruckus. In her admittedly sheltered life, she'd found it messy and not nearly as satisfying as masturbation.

He'd shown her how incredible her body could feel. How ineffectual her previous partners had been. It was a whole new ballgame with Nate, and yet…

If Nate did intend to sleep with her again, she would have to tell him no. It wasn't fair, and she wanted him like crazy, but she wouldn't be his distraction. She'd learn to live with her own failure somehow, but there would be no getting over being the cause of Nate's.

# 6

NATE SAT ON THE EDGE OF the bed in the room he'd taken for a month. No matter what, he wouldn't be signing up for another. His head dropped to his chest in exhaustion as he waited for Tam to finish in the bathroom.

It was after two-thirty in the morning and the team had talked over the plan until they all begged to go to sleep. It hadn't been enough. There were a great many things that had to go right for this to work. Every member of the team would have to do their part, and do it quickly. Their income would have been sharply curtailed, but damn if Vince and Kate hadn't saved the day. He'd objected to them throwing their savings into the pot, but they'd insisted.

He needed Tam and Kate to work here at the motel. He also needed computers for them to work on. And video equipment. He'd have to rent a machine shop, Harper and Tam would have to do some fancy chemistry and they'd all have to not get caught.

Boone, Seth and Cade needed to get inside that chamber. They needed to map out that whole building and figure out the electrical system.

He wiped a weary hand over his face then turned at the sound of the bathroom door opening.

Just looking at Tam calmed him down. He had a bunch of excuses for sharing this room with her but only one real reason. He wanted her. It was stupid and distracting and he knew better, but damnit, the idea of not having her in his bed wasn't acceptable.

She had changed into a long blue nightgown, one that had no sleeves, but had ruffles by her neck. It wasn't something he would have imagined her buying if she'd had a choice. She also looked sad again, depressed, and he instantly put his problems on the back burner. "Tam?"

"It's all yours," she said, stepping away from the bathroom door.

He would have liked a shower, but he wasn't about to leave now. "What's wrong?"

She looked at him pensively, as if she were deciding something important, then she joined him on the bed. She was so light, the mattress hardly dipped. "This isn't a good idea."

He sucked in a breath, afraid that if she tore apart the plan, he'd have to abandon it, and he had nothing else. "What, specifically?"

"You. Me. One bed."

It took him a moment to realize what she meant. He'd been thinking about this damn plan for days, but it hadn't coalesced until the drive up here. "I don't understand."

"I really loved making love with you, you know that, right?"

"I was sure up until about fifteen seconds ago."

Her smile hadn't always made him nuts. When he'd first seen her—nothing. Not a twinge, not a clue. It had changed somewhere along the line, but he had no idea why. He was absolutely certain, however, that if Tam smiled then asked him to run the circumference of the earth, he'd do it, or die trying.

"Come on," she said. "You were there, you know how incredible it was."

He looked into her almond-shaped eyes. Hell, she didn't even need to smile. "Yeah, I know."

"And I was there when you realized you'd forgotten to call Seth."

"It happens."

"To normal people. Not to you."

"So I'm not normal?"

"God, no," she said, and she sounded insulted. "You're an amazing man. An amazing leader."

"Thanks, I think."

"You should be thankful. You're not just saving our lives, but the lives of hundreds, maybe thousands of people."

"Tam, what's the issue here?"

"I'm a distraction. I don't mean to be, but it's clear I am. We can't afford any distractions. *Capisce?*"

"It's a real good argument, there, Tamara, but completely off base."

She leaned to the left and gave him one of her impatient looks. Back in the lab he'd gotten her a coffee pot, a treadmill and a hell of a lot of weird techno CDs all because of that look. "You turned completely cold and distant when you came back to the real world."

"Damn scientists never know when to ignore things."

"That wasn't a function of me being a scientist, dummy. Despite my lack of skills, I'm still a woman."

He grinned, he couldn't help it. That was one of the things that knocked him out about her. She thought she was a complete nerd. From top to toe. She was right, mostly. Except there was something else about her that had been calling to him for months.

He took her hand in his and met her gaze. "Sweetie, I haven't once been confused about your gender. You are the sexiest, most irresistible woman I've ever known."

She yanked her hand away. "Knock it off, Pratchett. I know all about your past exploits."

"Hey, that's not fair."

"You think we both came into this from a void? That we didn't have lives?"

"Things change."

"How many women have you been with since Kosovo?"

Man, she was brutal. "You. That's all."

"Given the circumstances, aren't you the least bit suspicious of your feelings about yesterday? That it may not have been the woman, but the event itself?"

"You think too goddamn much. I am not some kid who believes he'll die if he doesn't get some. I'm also experienced enough to recognize when something incredible happens in my life. Oddly, incredible doesn't happen very often. I was angry when I realized I hadn't checked in with the team. But I wasn't angry at you."

"Yes, you were."

"Okay, I was. But only for about an hour. Then I got my head out of my ass."

She grinned. "I'm trying as hard as I can not to picture that."

"Good. It was metaphorical."

"I realize."

"It was also the truth. Look, I may be making a huge mistake, but I don't think so. I relaxed more on the drive here than I have in maybe two years. I relaxed enough to pull together the plan that might save us all. I slept better, too. I'm going to need that kind of calm over the next month, more than ever. I don't mean to trivialize what happened between us, or make it all about me, but Tam, come on. If you're staying in another room, I won't be thinking about saving lives, I'll be thinking about you."

"Really?"

He gave her one of *his* impatient looks. "Do you think *I* want to die alone?"

Tam studied his face. Not the silly expression, but his eyes. She'd come to know some things about Nate, and she'd learned his expressive eyes gave him away. It's how she'd known that he wanted her. That only his strong values had kept him from coming on to her while he was her only contact. His eyes had let her know that her own decision to make love to him was a good one.

Now, this minute, he was unsure. He couldn't be certain that sharing a bed wasn't a mistake. Of course, she couldn't be certain that it wasn't the smartest thing they'd ever done. "All right," she said, "but on a trial basis. First time you screw up, I'm out of here. Got it?"

He leaned over and kissed her on the lips. "Deal." He brushed her cheek with the back of his hand. "I hope you won't take this the wrong way, but tonight, it's just sleep. I'm too damn tired to do anything else."

"The hell with that. You can't perform, I'm gone."

The look of shock on his face made her laugh. "Get over yourself, soldier. I can make it through one night without your hot lovin'."

"I'm a very tired man, and you're a very mean woman."

"No, I'm a very tired woman who's gone past exhaustion all the way to stupid. Go wash up. Don't be shocked if I've crashed before you return."

"Hot lovin'," he mumbled as he went to the bathroom. "Jeez."

She didn't feel all that wonderful about the sheets, the pillows or any other part of the room, but there really wasn't a choice—she needed to sleep.

It felt as if the invasion of the lab had happened weeks ago. Except for the sense memories. Those were new, something she'd never experienced before. Unlike normal memories, these came to her as a scent or a sensation—but each one dragged her instantly back. The cool metal of her weapon brought her face to face with the man who'd tried to kill her. The searing heat of the raging fire took her straight to the closet and the claustrophobic terror that she was trapped between death by fire or by gunshot.

If it was all the same to whoever was in charge, she'd rather skip the visceral associations. She got as comfortable as she could—relieved that the pillow didn't smell—and shut her eyes. The dip of the bed pulled her from the beginning of sleep, but she didn't mind. Not when she felt Nate's body at her back. His arm slipped around her waist. He spooned with her, and it was the first time in her life that she'd had the experience. She'd always thought it was terribly romantic when she'd read it in books. But the real thing? Heaven.

She wished she'd had the guts to sleep naked again, to feel him completely, but that was all she would have changed. With a deep sigh, she drifted once more. Safe.

CHRISTIE COMPLETELY UNDERSTOOD why they'd picked her. They'd discussed the subject all day. Harper couldn't go because she had to help Vince get the GHB. Kate couldn't go because she had to help Vince with acquiring the computers. Tam was out of the question. She was still too shaky from her narrow escape in L.A. But Christie, they'd reasoned, wasn't one of the original group. She hadn't known a thing about Kosovo until Omicron had come after her. She was the logical choice.

So she'd gotten all dolled up to go to the Renegade. Her mission was to flirt, to walk around, to get a clear shot of every man inside using the hidden camera in her purse strap. The camera was so tiny, she hadn't believed it would work until Boone showed her the image on the monitor.

Nate and Cade would be in the truck across the street from the bar. They'd make sure they had a good image of each guy, which Boone and Seth would then compare to the men with access to the chamber. When they found the right man, she'd get all dolled up again, go back to the Renegade when the subject was there, drug his drink and they'd steal his fingerprints. Easy as pie.

She was scared spitless.

Even before she'd been caught up in this mess, she'd never been one for bars. She wasn't much of a drinker, and small talk wasn't her forte, so there was a really good chance she could screw this up. Badly.

Boone had assured her she was totally up to the task, but then, he loved her. What else would he say? Harper had given her a few tips, reminding her to smile no matter what, to touch her hair a lot and that if she wanted someone to look at her face instead of her boobs she needed to touch their arm, then laugh.

Well, she couldn't stand in the parking lot forever. She took a deep breath then walked to the door. She could hear Alan Jackson on the jukebox. Once inside she realized just how loud the music was.

It was warm and crowded and so dark she worried that they wouldn't get even one clear picture. Not her problem. She got out a twenty and headed for the bar, adjusting her purse on her shoulder.

"Christie?"

She jerked at Nate's voice. In addition to the camera, she had a small receiver in her ear.

"Don't worry about the lighting," he said. "We've got it covered. As soon as possible, find yourself a seat at the bar. We need to make sure the camera is at the right angle."

She wasn't wearing a mike, so she just went ahead and did as he said. The bartender, tattooed and long haired, took her order, and then she turned to face the man on her right. He didn't seem like someone who'd be given top secret security clearance, but that wasn't her problem, either. "Hi."

"Hey. I haven't seen you here before."

"I'm new in town. I heard there was work out here that wasn't in a casino."

He nodded. Christie touched his arm, and laughed, sounding more like an idiot than a flirt. "I mean, if I have to serve one more drink…"

It worked like a charm. He looked her in the face, his smile hopeful, his eyes glassy from too much beer.

"We got it," Nate said. "Move on."

She turned back to the bar, looking for the bartender. He showed up, she took her beer and handed him the cash. Then she turned to the man on her left.

Now *he* looked like someone who might work for Omicron. He never smiled, he didn't even try to check out her boobs and if she hadn't spilled some beer on him, she wouldn't have gotten the shot.

It was a relief to stand after the all clear, but that moment of happiness slipped away as she gazed out at the crowded room. It was going to be a very long night.

NATE GOT BACK TO HIS ROOM at 3:00 a.m. They got a lot of faces on tape, but they wouldn't have results until Boone and Seth reviewed them.

For his part, all he wanted was to crawl into bed and hold Tam.

He still wasn't sure the arrangements were going to work out. This was their second night at Motel Sleaze, and they still hadn't made love.

From the look of things, they weren't going to tonight, either. Which, he hated to admit, was a relief. What he really needed was three days of nonstop sleep. It didn't help that every waking moment was filled with tension. There was so much to do, so few people to do it and they all had to hide like outlaws.

He looked at Tam, sleeping peacefully on her side of the bed, her hair still neat in a ponytail, her skin pale and perfect in the light from the john. He should wash up, brush his teeth, take off his clothes, but he couldn't seem to move. She'd become his anchor. His reason. Not that he didn't love his sister and care deeply about the rest of the team, but Tam was different. It shook him how badly he needed her to be okay. Nothing had panicked him as much as finding the lab torn apart. He'd seen a body seconds before the lab had blown up, and it could have been Tam. He'd raced to find her, but the anxiety had nearly crippled him. It was never to be mentioned, especially not to her, but there was no doubt in his mind that he would have lost it completely if she'd been killed. He'd have marched right into Omicron and murdered Leland Ingram with his bare hands.

Senator Raines would have loved that. He'd milk the publicity for all it was worth, making certain the public believed that Nate was not only a traitor to his country but also a cold-blooded killer.

He stretched his neck and moved his jaw as he headed for the bathroom. He felt like he'd aged twenty years in the last two. At least he had his friends and his sister right beside him. That was something to be grateful for. Tam was another.

She'd lived. That's what he needed to remember. Tam was alive. They'd made love, which had helped him remember why he was fighting so hard, and now there was a plan in motion to put this nightmare behind them.

It didn't take him long to wash and shave. Just as he was about to turn off the light, he heard Tam moan. When he got to the bed, she was still sleeping. She moaned again. He knew too well that she had a full range of nightmares in her beautiful head. But she wouldn't have to finish this one. He sat. Touched her arm lightly. "Tam. Honey?"

Practically vibrating with fright, her body was trembling and her breathing quick and shallow.

"Tam, wake up. You're okay. You're safe."

Her eyes shot open he took her up into his arms, holding her tightly.

"What happened?" she asked.

"You were having a nightmare."

"Is that all? You scared me."

He pulled away so he could see her. "Is that all?"

She nodded. "I'm sure you have them, too."

"That's not the point."

Tam gave him a crooked smile. "What is?"

"You shouldn't have bad dreams. Ever."

"Why not? I've had some pretty crappy things happen. I believe that we work stuff out in our dreams. Did you know in REM sleep, we have the exact same brain wave patterns as when we're awake?"

He kissed her, long and deep. Who else would look at nightmares as rationally as Tam? Chalk one up for the science geek.

Her arm went around his neck as the tip of her tongue brushed his lower lip. That was all it took. He moved away, got off the bed.

"What?"

"Too many clothes," he said, crouching to take off his boots.

"Good point." She threw back the covers and whipped off that staid, frilly nightgown.

He fumbled with his shoes some more because he couldn't look down. Not when she was right there in front of him, naked, small, elegant. The fatigue that had him practically sleepwalking two minutes ago was gone. So was his coordination. He teetered for a moment then sat on the floor. Hard.

Naturally, Tamara laughed.

He cursed, but he wasn't embarrassed or angry. Just happy she was okay. That they'd gotten through one more day without any injuries. At least he hoped so. Boone and Seth were still out there, risking it all.

"Hey, what happened?"

"I lost my balance." He got to his feet so he could get his jeans off.

"No, that's not what I mean. One minute you were smiling and silly, the next you weren't. What happened?"

He shook his head. "Nothing. It's not important."

Her head tilted to the side. "Wasn't it you who said we can only do what we can do?"

"Yeah."

"So tell me, Sergeant Pratchett. What can you do right now?"

He dropped his pants and his boxers, then whipped off his shirt as he toed off his socks. "I'm not exactly sure," he said. "Despite the fact that all I want is to ravish you until we're both comatose, I'm really afraid that I'll fall asleep at a very inappropriate time."

"Ravish me, huh?"

He nodded as he put one knee on the bed. Tam leaned her back against the wall as if they'd done this a hundred times but her nipples told a different story. They were hard and excited, just like his dick.

He moved next to her and maneuvered under the covers, so they both shared his pillow. Then he kissed her.

She ran her hand down his side, then up his back. Such a small hand. So delicate. Once more down his side, then she snuck it between them, and she touched his erection with her fingers.

He hissed at the sensation.

"Nate?"

"Yes?"

"You need to sleep. Let me just do this, okay? We'll make love tomorrow."

He shook his head. "No."

"Why not?"

"I want you to get off, too."

"I don't need to. This will make me happy."

He leaned back farther, barely able to see her expression in the dark. "That's crazy."

"No, it's not." She gripped his shaft firmly, then pumped, forcing his brain to short-circuit.

"It's what I want."

"But—"

She stopped him with a kiss. And got her way. In a shamefully short time, he felt the edge of his climax. She moved her hand more quickly and thrust her tongue deep into his mouth.

He came explosively, and when it was over, he drifted, barely aware that her lips were on his temple, that her breath was warm and sweet. Then, nothing.

# 7

BY NOON, VINCE HAD A LINE on four pretty decent computers that he could pick up in Vegas, had made a list of all the machine shops within a hundred miles and helped Kate find her green sweater, which, according to Kate, was the only sweater she truly loved. He'd also gone to the bank.

He'd talked to the branch manager privately, showing Mr. Eccles the badge he wasn't supposed to have and convincing Mr. Eccles that there was a very serious undercover mission afoot. It helped that back when Vince had quit the L.A.P.D., he'd stolen some letterhead from his ex-captain, upon which he'd written a letter about the serious undercover mission, and how Vince's identity had to be kept super-duper top secret. Not for the first time, it struck him that since he'd got together with Kate, he'd become a damn good criminal.

He'd made arrangements to get a large wire transfer from Los Angeles and to collect the money in cash. All of which would occur with absolutely no names involved. He'd left with a handshake and a jaunty salute.

He'd ducked yet another bullet. He'd made it out

without getting arrested, and no one, to the best of his knowledge, had followed him. He was so pleased he decided to make a pit stop before returning to Motel Hell. When he finally got there, he had to kick Christie's door to get her to let him in. His hands were full of pizza boxes and salads.

"You stopped?" Kate asked. "You stopped for pizza and you didn't even call me?"

"Hey, I brought you a salad. With mozzarella cheese in it."

She took the bag containing the salad and put it on the small round table, next to the very large boxes of pizza. Then she turned back to Vince and socked him in the arm.

"Ow." He rubbed where she'd hit him, regretting the time he'd encouraged her to work out. "That hurt."

"You should have called."

"Okay, okay. I will never get pizza again without calling first."

"It's not the—" She stopped. Looked at him through narrowed eyelids. "It's a good thing that you weren't killed on your way to the pizza place, or I would have—"

"Killed me? Again?"

"I would have managed it."

He took her beautiful face between his hands and kissed her. "I know you would have, sweetie. Can we eat now?"

She moved in for a kiss, but only bit his lower lip. "Now we can eat."

He checked, but she hadn't broken the skin. Which

meant he could safely put red pepper flakes on his slice of pepperoni pizza.

Christie, who'd ignored their little dance, had called the rest of the troops. Boone was up, but still groggy from his night behind the lines. Didn't stop him from taking a big old slice of pizza. By the time Vince had poured himself and Kate sodas, and grabbed a couple of pieces for himself, Seth, Harper, Cade, Nate and Tam had arrived.

Everyone was pleased about the luncheon menu. Milo, Christie's golden lab, sat next to Cade, who snuck him several pieces of pepperoni and sausage before his mom put a stop to it. Altogether, they were a happy bunch. Well, as happy as they ever got.

The minute lunch was done, Vince brought everyone up to speed. The computers would be in place in two days. There were several nearby machine shops that would fit their bill, and Kate had her green sweater.

He relaxed, knowing his job was done. He sipped cold soda as the others reported in. Christie's detail at the Renegade had gone well last night and now that Boone and Seth were there, they could begin going over the pictures of the patrons.

Harper had called an old friend, Noah somebody, who agreed to deliver the GHB. She gave Seth a curious look, and they'd both stared at his claw.

"You'll meet him somewhere else," Nate said.

Harper turned from Seth. "He's safe. He's the guy who gave Seth his prosthesis."

"I don't care. We can't compromise the motel. When's he coming?"

"Tomorrow or Wednesday," she said. "He's got to spend some time with Seth, check him out."

"Good. We need to be in perfect working order." He leaned back on the couch and put his arm around Tam. Not on her shoulders directly, but on the couch above her shoulders.

Vince wasn't sure what was going on between the two of them. Kate had been mysterious about it, smiling as if it were a secret a dumb cop like him couldn't grasp. Vince just figured they were testing the relationship waters. It seemed to be a disease among the team. Go into hiding, narrowly escape something horrible, find the love of your life.

His gaze moved over to Cade, and there it was again. Because Vince was still a cop at heart, he'd noticed before that Cade had some kind of weird thing going on about Nate and Tam. From the moony looks he gave when he thought he wouldn't get caught, Vince figured Cade had a crush on the petite chemist.

It must be hard for him, going solo among all these couples. He'd have to ask Kate more about him. She'd already told him that Cade had left a fiancée behind. Rough. And he always made time for a five mile run sometime during the day. Even if he'd been out all night on patrol. Now that, Vince didn't get at all. Sure, physical fitness was great and important, but shit. The guy got enough exercise hiding from people who wanted to kill him. Hey, that would make for an interesting fitness plan. Instead of hiring a personal trainer, hire a hit man.

At the moment, Nate and Tam were more interesting than Cade, so he went back to watching them. Yep, there was definitely something going on between those two, but he'd wager they hadn't figured out what. They were too hesitant with each other, always checking to make sure a look or a touch was welcome.

Vince had no doubt that whatever was holding them back here wasn't holding them back in the bedroom.

There was no room for that particular kind of indecision, not living under a death sentence. Everything became more intense. Jeez, he and Kate were doing it like bunnies. Of course, that probably had more to do with how crazy he was about Kate than the danger.

Last night, after one of their bunny sessions, Kate had asked him if he would go back to being a cop after it was all over. He hadn't been able to answer her. Not definitively. He was leaning toward no. The only thing he knew with certainty was that he'd be with Kate. Nothing was going to change that.

"Hold on," Boone said. "I'll be right back." He got up from his perch on the floor and went into the bedroom. When he came back, he had two canisters in his hand. They were made of metal with a warning on the side. As he read, Vince's heart sped up and he grabbed Kate's hand to get her the hell away.

"It's okay," Boone said. "These are empty. New. They've never contained any of the gas."

"You could have said something before you got them," Vince said, controlling his anger. Damn it, those fucking ex-soldiers. They were worse than undercover cops.

Nate took one of the canisters and shook his head

over the symbols and the wording. The canister itself was heavy, made of thick aluminum. On one side was the skull and crossbones and the word *Poison,* on the other was a chart, a diamond broken into four quadrants of red, yellow, white and blue. Each quadrant had a one or a zero. There was nothing else, no manufacturer's name, no ID of the gas itself. It could have been any chemical weapon, and if the canister was found by the media or an environmental group, they would assume it was from an already existing stockpile.

As Nate went over the plan for the canisters, Vince studied Tam. He'd only met her a few days ago, but he'd heard plenty. Kate had told him she was smart as hell, and that she'd figured out the antidote to the gas, even though she'd had to compile notes from about eight different scientists. She sure as hell didn't look like a brainiac.

Interesting about her and Nate. It was a good match for the moment, but he doubted very much it would stand the test of freedom. Nate was one hell of a leader and a man he'd follow to the end, but he was not a one-woman man. Now, yes, but when his options broadened? When the ladies found out what a hero he was?

Vince knew guys like Nate, although he had a suspicion that his friend here didn't leave furious women behind. No, he'd tell them the truth and they'd thank him for enriching their lives.

Kate poked him in the ribs. "Hey, damn it. Did you even hear the question?"

"Yeah, I… No. What was it?"

"Can you handle the machine shops?" Nate sounded calm, but it was real clear that Vince better not do any more wool gathering. "They can't be local. And we need about a dozen canisters just like this in about two weeks."

"Yeah, I can handle that. But won't they get suspicious when they see that skull and crossbones?"

"We'll handle the markings ourselves. All they have to do is duplicate the canisters."

"Check. I'll get on it ASAP."

Nate leaned back and took a quick peek at Tam. She smiled and Vince could see the man relax. When Nate turned back to Seth and Boone, he was cool as a cucumber. "What about it, guys? You ready to look at pictures?"

LELAND INGRAM STARED out the jet's window, letting the dark sea quiet his mind. He'd thought the trip to Grand Cayman would have done the trick, but he'd had a hell of a time relaxing.

Everything was going so well. They already had a number of foreign buyers lined up who were willing to pay the exorbitant prices they were charging for the gas. The morons were so anxious to kill off their enemies that they hardly listened when he told them one canister of the gas was enough to kill tens of thousands of people if properly dispersed. Of course, Ingram didn't believe for a second the gas would be handled according to the Material Safety Data Sheet. More than likely, those who bought the weapon would die right alongside those they wanted to kill. It worked for him.

What his buyers also didn't know was that the payload per canister was a quarter of what was advertised. They didn't want all of say, South Africa, to be wiped out. That would bring too much attention to their gambit. The goal was to generate in excess of one billion dollars after expenses. The money would be used judiciously in the War on Terror. Senator Raines might have a lot of faults, but his vision was pure.

Ingram didn't see a need to make any more gas than was necessary. Once the stockpile was gone, they would dismantle the plant and make sure that anyone who could someday develop a guilty conscience was paid off or eliminated. Omicron would go back to its main business of consulting, and no one would be the wiser.

Only one thing stood in the way of his success. Those damn soldiers and the women who'd stuck their noses where they didn't belong. He had to get Tamara Chen in custody. Of those who could spoil his plans, there was none more dangerous than her. She had the right credentials, she understood the nature of the gas. She had to be taken. She had to be killed. The problem was, he had no idea where she was.

She couldn't have left the country, not by any conventional means. He'd personally seen to it that she was placed on the no-fly list and her picture sent out to every CIA and FBI office in the country identifying her as a home grown terrorist affiliated with Al Queda.

"Sir, would you care for another drink?"

He looked over at the stewardess, a lovely young thing hired by the firm that maintained the private jet. "Coffee," he said.

She smiled as she turned back to the galley, and he wondered if Raines had anything to do with her being on board. Ingram knew about the man's philandering, and despised that side of him. But Raines didn't welcome any personal conversation, let alone advice about the importance of family.

He turned back to the window, but he wasn't looking at the ocean any longer. His mind was too busy with the plan he had hatched in an inspired second. By the time he finished his coffee, he knew exactly what he was going to do to flush Dr. Chen out of hiding.

SETH WAITED IN THE TRUCK for Harper to check them into a room. He stared at the casino on his right, and the one across the street. He'd never been to Mesquite, Nevada before, and hadn't realized it was a miniature Las Vegas. Although, looking at the license plates, this town seemed to cater to the locals. There were one hell of a lot of RVs in the parking lot, even though it was still winter.

It had been Noah who'd suggested they meet at the Virgin River Hotel. He'd stayed there before, and he thought it would be quiet and private enough. And it was the only place in town that had a movie theater.

He'd like to do that—go to the movies. Buy some popcorn and put his arm around Harper as they watched the big screen. He had no idea what was playing. He couldn't remember the last time he'd glanced at the Calendar section of the *Times*. Entertainment for him was being alone with Harper. They hardly ever even turned on the TV.

He looked back at the hotel entrance, and there she was, looking beautiful in a white sweater and slacks. Her confidence always amazed him. She held her head high, her back straight, not noticing the glances she got from men and women alike.

She had become an amazing partner. They still had their moments. She was stubborn and so was he. But mostly, they fit each other. It made all the difference.

"Room 6110," she said, as she got into the truck. "I'll call Noah once we're inside."

He drove around the huge parking lot, past the pool and the long two-story buildings surrounding the casino proper.

They were in the farthest building, in the back, on the first floor. Excellent. There were only two other cars parked there, and the room she'd got was far from both.

Once parked, he grabbed their duffel bags from the back, and they went inside. It was nothing great, but a hell of a lot nicer than their home base.

First thing he did was get out his bug scanner. There was no way anyone could have known they were coming here, to this room, but he'd grown accustomed to being exceptionally cautious.

Harper called Noah on her cell, giving him only the necessary information. He was already in Vegas, so he'd meet them in under two hours.

The room was clean, and so was the phone. Seth looked at his watch then met Harper's gaze. Her smile told him they were on the same page. There was at least an hour to kill and a king-sized bed. Waste Not, Want Not.

IT WAS TEN-THIRTY, and for once, Nate was in the room, in the bed, not asleep. Tam looked at him again, just to make sure he hadn't drifted off, but no, he was still watching TV. He had a beer on the nightstand, which he sipped periodically, and the remains of a turkey sandwich on a plastic plate.

There were things happening here, things that felt important. Just for starters the fact that he muted the commercials. All of them. Even when he was eating or drinking, his free hand was on the remote. Then there was the whole gun prep thing. Jeez. Before dinner, he'd sat at the small round table and cleaned his weapon so carefully she wondered if he had a touch of obsessive-compulsive disorder. Or maybe he'd just been in the military too long. He'd smiled in this possessive, affectionate way when he'd finished, and it would have creeped her out if she hadn't needed him to protect her.

But the most interesting thing was the touching part. She was in a T-shirt and panties. He was in his boxer shorts, ever able to leap to the door if something came up. From the moment he'd come in from a meeting with Vince, some part of his body had touched some part of her body.

When she'd been making the sandwiches, it had been his hip. When she'd taken off her pants, his hand went to the small of her back. In bed, they were thigh to thigh, and when she rolled to get her drink, he touched her shoulder.

All that, and she didn't think he wanted to do anything but this. Watch the tube, then go to sleep.

Was this normal? Not the TV or the sleep part. Did all new couples touch like this? She liked it, no question about that. After such a long time alone, it felt terrific. But that didn't mean it was healthy.

"Nate?"

He turned his head toward her, but kept his gaze on the TV. "Yeah?"

"What do you miss most?"

That got his full attention. "About what?"

"Your life?"

His thumb moved from the mute button to the on-off button and the room became quiet. "Most? I'm not sure."

"What are the contenders?"

"My work."

"You really like all that stuff, huh? The guns, the danger. But then, you've got that in this life, too."

"That's not the part I miss. It's hard to explain if you haven't been in the service. I liked the challenge, the fact that I wouldn't know from day to day what we were going to face. And the camaraderie. I don't think there's any situation around where men depend on each other so thoroughly, and when the pressure's off, man, the partying…"

She grinned. "I can only imagine. My colleagues at MIT sucked at partying. They'd all have to talk shop, and after two beers, they wanted to go home."

"Well, when this is over, me and the boys will show you how."

"You're on. But what else?"

"I miss feeling safe."

"That one I completely understand."

"I'm lucky Christie's here, even though I wouldn't have wanted this for her."

Tam felt the twist in her gut that had become too familiar. "I miss my parents. I miss them so much."

"Tell me about them," he said.

She closed her eyes, picturing her mother as if she'd seen her yesterday. "My mother's family is from Canada. Toronto, actually. She met my father when she was on vacation in San Francisco. He was working his way through school as a tour guide. He grew up speaking Cantonese, so it was an easy job for him."

"So, she was on one of his tours?"

Tam nodded. "By mistake. Even though she didn't understand much of what he said, she stayed for the whole ride. Afterward, my father repeated the trip in English, just for her."

"And your father's a physicist, right?"

"Yes. He teaches. Writes. And my mother teaches, too. Education was a very big hairy deal in my family."

"Good thing you inherited the beauty and the brains."

She eyed him, letting him know she wasn't buying the corny line. "My mother warned me about guys like you."

"Really? What did she say?"

Tam sighed. "Mostly she told me that men like you didn't go out with girls like me."

"What did she mean?"

"Somehow my mother, who, by the way, has honey-blond hair, evolved into the ultimate Chinese wife. Overprotective, superstitious, and completely convinced that after I graduated with honors from MIT, I should find a nice man like my father and focus all my attention on giving her grandsons."

"She must have really loved your going to Kosovo."

Tam remembered the day she'd told her family. Her father had asked her if she was determined to go. When she said yes, he'd gotten very quiet. Probably because her mother was talking enough for both of them. "I wish I'd handled it better," she said. "I didn't know it was going to be the last time I'd see them."

"It's not," Nate said. He caressed her cheek with his fingers. "I wish there was a way for you to see them."

"I know there isn't, but I hate it."

"Yeah, me too."

"Uh, try that again? You sound awfully insincere."

He smiled and dropped his head. "Yeah, well, I do miss them. We just never had that great of a relationship."

"Christie said something about your father being sick?"

"He's got Alzheimer's, and that's brutal."

"How's your mother?"

"She's consistent, if nothing else. The whole world revolves around my mother. Everything's personal, and no one understands. When we were kids she tried to be a loving mother, but the pretense wore on her. Finally, when Christie was in high school, she stopped pretending. Everyone was relieved. It had been too much work."

"Even so—"

"Even so," he said, "I do miss her. I miss my old college friends, even though we hardly got to see each other. I miss going to football games."

"Football?"

"Go Army."

"Right."

"MIT has a football team, doesn't it?" he teased.

"Probably. Didn't we have the whole I'm a nerd conversation?"

He nodded. "So, what do you miss most?"

"Well, I already said. My folks."

"What else?"

"My illusions."

He shifted more, so he looked at her straight on. "Meaning?"

"Before this, I had all kinds of grandiose dreams about my future. I was going to win a Nobel. I was going to cure cancer. I would be the alumni of the year. Oh, and I'd own a really cool car."

Nate laughed. "I'd love to know what kind of car you consider really cool."

"A Bentley. Silver. With every extra possible."

"A Bentley? Jeez, you are a nerd."

She sat up straighter and gave him an evil look. "Excuse me. Bentleys are excellent cars. They're very classy."

"A Ferrari is a cool car. A 'Vette is cool. A Bentley's for your grandfather."

"You know nothing of class. I'm appalled. With all your world travels, you're just a heathen."

"Heathen? Nah. Barbarian, maybe."

"Just please don't tell me you think classical music is boring and that you'd rather go blind than go to a museum."

He looked at her funny. "Museum? I've heard of Mooseums, where they got all them cows—"

She laughed, and so did he and it was the nicest, most normal conversation she'd had in forever. He scooted closer to her, put his arm around her shoulders, then turned the TV back on. Just like real people.

CHRISTIE HAD GONE TO THE Renegade five nights in a row, and they hadn't yet found the right subject. Nate was beginning to think that Omicron made their top level employees sign a nonfraternization agreement. But, they'd still keep trying. He'd been in Christie's bedroom, where they'd set up the computer, as Boone, Seth and Christie combed through yet another night's take, but he'd had to move, to stretch his legs so he could think.

There were just so damn many things that could go wrong. Tam had told him to focus on everything that had gone right in the last two weeks, but his brain didn't work that way. In fact, the only thing that had taken his mind off disaster scenarios had been Tam herself.

Jesus, she was… He shook his head at the way his shoulders relaxed at the mere thought of her. It worked every time.

The woman helped him forget everything—that there was even a world outside their bed. She'd really gotten into it, wanting to explore different positions, not to mention some sex games she'd heard of. Just last night she'd asked him to blindfold her, to tie her up. He'd been hesitant—bondage was fun when the world around you was safe, but when she was in this much danger?

Turned out, she must have felt pretty safe with him because she didn't freak at all. In fact, she'd been so goddamn hot, he'd gotten it up twice in, like, three hours. Considering that most of the time he felt as old as Methuselah, it was a pleasant change.

Shit. Just picturing how she'd looked tied to the chair

made him hard. He'd pulled her to the edge of the seat and kept her legs spread wide, giving him ample access to her pussy. To say she'd been surprised when he'd shaved her was an understatement.

He'd lathered her up and as he slowly divested her of her dark curls, he'd watched her swell before his eyes. By the time she was clean and smooth as silk, she was breathing so hard he had to keep checking to make sure she wouldn't hyperventilate. She'd also begged him to do something, anything, to ease her need.

Bastard that he was, he'd made her wait on that. Oh, he'd teased her with his tongue, taking her right to the edge, then he'd changed his tactics, feeling wicked when she'd begged and begged.

He'd offered her his cock, and she'd sucked him with every intention of making him lose his mind. But he was a soldier and he'd been tested before. It had taken everything he had to pull out before he came, but the payoff was worth it.

It still amazed him how beautiful she'd looked, even when he couldn't see her eyes. He had to admit he'd been somewhat obsessed with those until last night when he'd really studied the rest of her face.

Her lips were smooth and pink, not too thin, but not ridiculously puffed up. Then there was her pale skin, almost translucent and a shocking contrast to her dark, nearly black hair.

The feel of her skin always lingered, and when he closed his eyes he could remember the tactile pleasure so well it was almost as good as the real thing. But from now on, he'd add her voice to his memories, combining the warm silk of her cheek with the sound of her pleading to come.

He adjusted his cock, sorry now that he'd let his mind wander away from the business at hand.

But damned if he could push away the image of the moment he'd balanced his knees on the pillows. She'd still been tied to the chair, unable to move more than a couple of inches, still blindfolded, with her senses on full alert.

He'd been so hard it hurt, but he'd taken his time getting his position just right. Then he'd gripped the edges of her chair and thrust inside her so hard, both of them had nearly toppled.

Her scream had probably awakened everyone at the motel, but since the only residents were his people, he didn't care.

Tam had come so fast it stunned him, and he hadn't been far behind. It had been hell untying her, but as he well knew, there was nothing more uncomfortable than being bound after the main event.

She still had tears in her eyes when he'd taken off the blindfold and that panicked him, but she'd kissed him, held him, trembled in his arms.

He shook himself out of the memory, trying hard to remember that he had a mission to plan. He adjusted his cock again but it was pretty useless. There was nothing to do but take his shirt out of his pants, hoping no one exited the bedroom before he'd shrunk.

His phone rang. He got it out of his pocket and saw it was Eli. Just as he answered, Boone, Seth and Christie came out of the bedroom, and he could tell they'd found the perfect subject. He couldn't celebrate yet. He turned his back on the trio and listened carefully to what Eli had to say. The conversation was brief but it made the hairs on the back of his neck stand up and every other part of him deflate.

He hung up and took a moment before he turned.

The three of them must have picked up on his mood because they were all silent and staring.

"That was Eli," he said. Even as he spoke, his anger and frustration rose so fast his hands curled into fists and he could feel the pulse at his temple throb. "A village in Chad has been wiped out by that damn gas! Over six hundred deaths at last count. Men, women, children."

# 8

TAM WAS MORE WORRIED ABOUT Nate than she was about the kidnapping. The two of them plus Harper were sitting in an abandoned warehouse outside of Overton, a tiny town between Vegas and Mesquite. They'd bought a gurney from a hospital supply store in Vegas, some arc lights on stands from a movie production supplier and the Mikrosil from a friend of Vince's. The copy machine had been bought at Staples.

Christie was at the Renegade right now slipping a dose of GHB into Rodney Hammond's drink. Then she would entice him outside on the premise of getting lucky. By the time they reached the truck, Rodney would already feel the effects of the drug. He might struggle, but not very strongly.

But back here, there was nothing to do but wait. Nate checked his watch for the fifth time in as many minutes. He hadn't wanted her here, but she knew her presence would have a calming effect on him. He'd gone berserk when he'd found out about the deaths in Chad. Not in front of his team, of course. But when he'd come back to their room, he'd thrown around a few choice items, only one of which wasn't plastic, and it had taken her a while to find out why.

Her heart had sunk when he told her what Eli had said. It brought home too clearly that they had to succeed, and do it damn soon.

As for her, she'd barely made it to the bathroom before she'd gotten sick.

After she'd cleaned up, she'd opened the bathroom door to find Nate on the bed, his head in his hands, and he was shaking. He never trembled—not that she'd seen—not even the night of the lab attack.

She'd put aside her own troubles and gone to him. She wasn't important now. He was. Nate was their last hope, and he couldn't fall apart, not when there was so much to do.

"You want some tea?"

Tam jumped at Harper's voice, brought back from her memories to the warehouse.

Nate shook his head in response to Harper's soft question. "No, thanks."

"Okay, then, will you stop looking at your watch? It's making me nuts."

He gave Harper a grim smile, and held off. At least for awhile. When he checked again, Tam got up, moved her chair to the other side of his and held his hand.

"Sneaky," he said.

"Practical. We need Harper to be sharp when they get here. She can't be wanting to punch your lights out."

"I never understood the reluctance to have women in combat," he said. "You're all ruthless."

Harper snorted. And then they heard the truck.

Nate was on his feet so fast he nearly knocked his

chair over. But then Harper seemed just as anxious. Tam was, too, she just had her focus on Nate, not the mission. That, she knew would be successful. The team was too good to screw it up.

Nate had his weapon out, pointing at the loading dock door as it screeched open. He put it down the moment he saw Boone.

Seth drove in, and there was Rodney in the truck bed, sleeping. At least Tam hoped it was just sleep.

Harper climbed up beside him with her medical bag. While she checked his vitals, Nate and Seth set up the lights. In the meantime Cade mixed half a tube of white Mikrosil and half a tube of hardener in a bowl. After they were given the okay, the guys lifted Rodney—who wasn't a small man—off the truck and onto the gurney. He didn't seem the type to have attracted a woman as gorgeous as Christie. He must have thought he'd died and gone to heaven when she suggested they leave the bar.

Even Tam had to admit Christie had done her part well. She was in tight jeans, a low-cut blouse, and her makeup was perfect. She'd probably outclassed everyone in the joint. Not to mention making Tam feel as though she could win a grunge competition.

She turned back to check on Nate, who seemed a lot better now that he was finally doing something. She felt as if she were in an operating room. Everyone hovering around the subject as Cade put Rodney's elbow in a sling so that his hand was elevated.

Cade used a wooden mixing stick to slather the putty on the man's hand, starting several inches below the wrist. It didn't take all that long as he didn't want it to dry unevenly, but it felt like hours to Tam.

Finally, it was done. Now they had to wait at least twenty minutes for the stuff to dry.

Nate turned his attention immediately to Rodney's wallet. There was no keycard, but there was an ID card, which he took over to the color copier they'd hooked up to a portable generator.

He made a dozen copies. As the clock ticked, Harper used a scalpel to cut out Rodney's picture. When she finished with one, she handed it to Boone, who replaced the photo with one of himself. Then Nate took the fake ID and ran it through the copier again, only this time the machine laminated the card. Christie trimmed the new ID. All of this was done in silence; everyone intent on not making even the smallest mistake.

They made one ID for each member of the team. They didn't bother to change the name. If someone looked that closely, they'd realize immediately that it was fraudulent.

She found herself pacing, wishing they'd given her an assignment. As Nate had proven once again, it was always easier to work than wait.

The deaths in Chad would haunt them all. But the news had also reinforced their determination. Not only that. The news had accelerated their timeline. They had to move fast. As fast as they could. No one wanted another village wiped out.

"Time," Nate said.

They had finished the whole set of IDs, all except the final trim, but Christie abandoned her task to watch Cade's next move.

He touched the cast in a bunch of places, particularly between the fingers. He must have been satisfied because he loosened the putty around the wrist, then took hold of the molded plastic and pulled it off the hand, inside out. When he was finished he had a perfect glove. Even Tam could see the ridged prints.

Harper used some alcohol pads to clean up Rodney's hand. Then she checked his vitals again, and his eyes. "I don't know how long he'll be out. But he won't remember any of this."

"Tam, Harper and Christie, you take care of things in here," Nate said before turning to his men. "Let's load him up and get him back to his car." He replaced Rodney's wallet and they hoisted him into the truck bed.

Boone and Seth got in the front and Cade stayed in the bed. Nate checked outside, then gave them the go-ahead. The truck headed out slowly over the broken concrete outside.

Rodney would wake up sometime in the next few hours, wondering what the hell had happened. By then, all evidence that the team had been in the warehouse would be gone. They'd each have an ID card, giving them level four clearance, and one set of fingerprints that would change everything.

NOW THAT THE COMPUTERS HAD arrived, Tam found that her last three days were a lot like those she'd spent in the lab. No experiments, but long stretches of solitary work, broken up by lunch with whoever happened to be at the motel. Her assignment was to type in the data she'd compiled about the gas and the antidote. To make the heavy scientific jargon understandable to the layman. Everything had to be recorded, every trial and every observation. She kept putting off transcribing the notes of her failed dispersal system, but that would have to be included, too.

What made it all bearable were her nights. Although technically, it was her mornings. Nate worked so late he'd come to their room well past midnight. Despite his exhaustion, they made love, which saw them through the next twenty-four hours.

She saved her page and got up from the little round table. They didn't have much in what passed for a kitchen, but she had her stock of Diet Pepsi Lime and he had his Corona. The beverages filled most of the refrigerator, but there was also a loaf of bread and peanut butter in there, too. She wished it were tomorrow.

Tonight, Boone and Seth were going to enter the chamber using Rodney's fingerprints. The tension had the whole team on edge, and she found it safer to lock herself away and concentrate on her work. Nate, however, couldn't lose himself in formulas. Although he didn't carry out the missions, he felt the weight of each and every one.

The day after they'd made the mold of Rodney's hand, Nate had gone with Vince to the machine shop. She'd been completely terrified until he'd walked back through their door, and that memory helped her be patient when he was gruff, or when he paced across the small room for hours at a time.

He held them all on his shoulders.

Just as the fizz of her soda was dying down there was a knock on her door. It frightened her as it always did, but she let her training take over. She went to the bedside table and took her weapon out from the drawer. She released the safety as she crossed the room, and only then did she look through the peephole. It was Seth.

"You busy?"

"Just pouring myself a soda. Want one?"

He nodded as he entered and didn't blink when she put her gun back in the drawer. "I've had so much coffee my eyes have turned brown."

She laughed, having noticed his striking green-gold eyes the first time they'd met. "What's up?" she asked as she poured his soda.

"Not much. Can't sleep, of course, and I'm annoying the crap out of Harper so I thought I'd come here."

"And annoy the crap out of me?"

"Yep."

"Thanks. I could use a little distraction."

He sat down in the chair by the table and she took her drink and sank to the floor in front of the bed. "How are you two doing?"

"Fine," she said. "Why?"

He studied the plastic glass. "Just thought I'd check in. Nate's about the best man I know, but…"

"Go on."

"He's never been too keen on the whole relationship thing."

"Ah. Well, I know that about him. Kate warned me."

"So you know that you guys are probably not going to, uh—"

"You mean he hasn't told you?"

Seth looked at her. "What?"

"That we're getting married."

His claw opened and shut, which Tam figured was an involuntary muscle spasm, although she wasn't all that familiar with the way the prosthesis worked. "You are?"

"I suppose I should have waited for him to tell you," she said, keeping a straight face. "It won't be a big wedding, but you guys will all be invited."

"Shit. Really? He never said anything. Does Christie know?"

"Seth, I appreciate the talk, I do, but please don't worry. We're not getting married or even going steady. We're taking each day as it comes."

He frowned, and she could see why Harper was always touching him. He was a good looking guy, almost as handsome as Nate. "That wasn't nice."

"No, I suppose it wasn't, but I warned you I was bored."

He drank some soda and made a little face. "What is this?"

"Lime."

"Oh, okay."

"Seth?"

"Yeah?"

"Was that it? Just a general warning not to fall head over heels for the sergeant?"

"Pretty much. You know the girls. They just—"

"The girls? So it's not just Harper, but Kate and Christie, too?"

He nodded a little guiltily.

"Why are they worried about me?"

"I don't know. I told them you weren't a kid, but they wanted to make sure no one would get hurt."

"No one," she said, under her breath, "meaning me. You're right, I'm not a kid."

"Hey, we didn't want to upset you, either. This is difficult enough without hurt feelings."

"I'm curious," she said. "Did you draw the short straw?"

"No. I volunteered. I've been with Nate through a lot. I've never seen him intentionally mislead anyone. But he always kept things short and sweet, you know?"

She studied him, sure he was telling her the truth, not just about Nate but about his motives. "Tell me about him."

"What do you mean?"

"What's he like when it isn't the end of the world?"

Seth leaned back in his chair, his claw resting in his lap, his other hand around the glass. He was in the uniform they'd all adopted—jeans, boots, T-shirts. It was still cold as hell out, but his jacket wasn't built for warmth. She knew he had a weapon on him, probably at the small of his back. They were always wary and always prepared. "Well, he was good for a laugh."

"Nate?"

Seth nodded. "Everyone wanted to hang out with him. Even senior officers. I won't lie to you, he liked to party. There's not a mission we've had where he didn't know the hours of the nearest bar."

"Kate told me he was much hankered after."

He grinned. "Nice way of putting it. But yeah, the

ladies always found him. The rest of us got his castoffs."
He shook his head. "To add insult to injury, he never
lost at pool. Not once. He went up against some damn
good players, too."

"I don't believe it."

"I was there. The man knows how to play eight ball."

"I meant about you getting his castoffs."

Oh, she'd made him blush. How interesting. Big,
tough Seth, who'd killed a man with his claw, and he
was shy. She wouldn't have guessed.

"I did okay. But I was outclassed."

"What about when he wasn't in a bar. Did he talk
much about his family?"

"Just Christie. We all knew about her. His folks? I
don't know the whole story, but I don't think they got
along too well."

That jibed with what she'd picked up. "He's good at
what he does, isn't he?"

"The best. He's saved my life more than once. I'd
follow him all the way through hell."

"I think we're there, don't you?"

His head dipped down for a long moment, and when
he looked at her again it was with that same fierceness
she often saw on Nate's face. "He'll get us through."

"I believe you."

After another pause, he finished off his drink in a
couple of gulps then stood. "I think Harper's been
without annoyance for too long." He headed to the door
and opened it slowly, looking down to the parking lot.

"Seth?"

He turned.

"It's going to last for you two, isn't it?"

His smile changed his face. "Yeah. It's for keeps."

"Good. That's really good."

"Hang in there, Tam. It'll be over soon."

"One way or another."

"Think good thoughts," he said, as he slipped outside and closed the door behind him.

She didn't go back to work. She didn't even stand up. Seth had told her a great deal in a short time, most of it unspoken. It would be wise for her to think things through.

Nate was an easy man to love, even for experienced women. She was nothing of the sort. He had taken her places she'd never dreamed of, all without leaving the room. She admired him, she liked him and loving him was only an inch away.

The problem was, if she continued making love to him, would she be strong enough to let him go?

It was just past 2:00 a.m. and most of the staff in the processing plant were on break. Including Rodney Hammond.

Seth and Boone were in the full contamination gear required to enter the chamber. The face mask was a self-contained breathing apparatus, which not only had one canister of oxygen worn on the back, but an auxiliary unit in case the first canister failed. The only skin left uncovered was Boone's hand, encased in its putty glove.

They approached the hand scanner casually, as if they belonged there, but they were on full alert. Next to the chamber door were huge warning signs. Evacuation routes were illustrated on a plaque, but Seth knew if it got to that there would be no time to escape. If anything went wrong, they were toast, but at least they wouldn't live to be interrogated.

Boone put his hand on the screen, and Seth held his breath. He thought about Harper, and how worried she was about this. He'd tried to tell her it would be okay, that all they were doing was getting a lay of the land in the inner chamber, but she hadn't been reassured.

She knew too well what death by Omicron's gas was like. It was worse for her even than for Christie, because Harper had witnessed the devastating effects with her own eyes in Serbia.

Boone's hand with Rodney's fingerprints were scanned, and time slowed as they waited for the red button to turn green. If it didn't? They'd have to figure out another way in. If it did? He wasn't sure he wanted to find out.

It turned green. Rodney Hammond, who was most likely still wondering what the hell had happened to that gal at the Renegade, had come through like a champ.

The two men stepped up to the thick metal doors which slid open without a sound.

Inside, the room looked blue. It was the vapors from the cooling system, swirling in the air. On either side of a long walkway marked with vivid yellow paint were rows of stacked bomb casings. There must have been five hundred bombs in the room, each of them with a payload of instant death. Whoever bought them would need to launch them, either from a plane or from a stationary launcher, but the effect would be the same. They would rise into the sky and then a small explosion would crack the bomb casing and the container storing the gas. As the gas floated down everything it touched would die. Birds, insects, trees, fish. The people would be gone in agonizing minutes.

The men stepped inside and the door closed behind them. Seth wanted nothing more than to get the job done and get out. He shivered, and he wondered if it was the cold, or the fact that this place existed at all.

The two of them followed the yellow line, counting canisters as they walked. Seth pulled his small notebook out of his glove and began his diagram. The break would be over in ten minutes. He wanted to be finished in nine.

# 9

THE GUYS RETURNED TO THE motel at 5:45 a.m. Every member of the team was up and waiting for them in Christie and Boone's room.

Nate studied both men. They looked weary as hell, the tension still etched in pale faces but he could see the iron beneath. They'd gotten the job done, as he'd expected.

Boone handed him his notebook. Nate put it in his pocket and shook his friend's hand. "Good job."

"It's big and it's tight. It won't be a cakewalk."

Nate had expected nothing less. "It can be done?"

"Damn straight."

Seth came up behind Boone and gave his notebook over. "Anybody else want a beer?"

Nate grinned. He'd heard those words so many times it had become a ritual between them. No matter how close they'd come to cashing out, when the last bullet had been fired, they shared a beer. That it was just after dawn didn't faze him. "Sounds good."

Seth shook his hand, which was also part of the routine, then he pulled him close in a hell of a bear hug. It was all Nate could do not to grunt as Seth's enthusiasm overrode his typical caution with his metal prosthetic. Nate would have a bruise, not that he gave a shit.

Christie and Harper went with the men into the kitchen to get the beers. He sat down next to Tam on the floor, leaving the couch to the victors. It was something of a surprise to see them bring back beers for everyone, but it felt right. They needed to celebrate every victory as a team. He glanced at Tam, knowing she didn't care much for Corona, but she smiled and took hers without a blink.

Vince and Kate were sitting by the kitchen on the floor. Cade was grinning, despite the fact that his companion was Milo. Christie sat very close to Boone on the couch so that Seth and Harper could squeeze in, too.

When they were all settled, Nate lifted his bottle. "Here's to good friends and a mission well done." He drank, and the morning beer tasted about as good as a liquid gets. His team was safe.

His arm went around Tam's shoulder and she settled into his side. He watched her for awhile, as she celebrated with the rest of them, and yeah, she was part of the crew now. He felt good with her beside him in a way that he'd never experienced before.

The women he'd been with had been fun and sexy and he missed them all, but they'd been bonus points. Sometimes he got lucky, sometimes he didn't, but he never spent a moment wishing for more.

He knew his feelings about Tam were connected to the circumstance and that he'd come to see her as more than just a brilliant woman, but as his good luck charm. Crazy, yeah, but he didn't care. She was special. Special as hell.

"So tell us about it," Christie said.

Boone looked at Nate, who figured they all had an equal amount to lose so why not know the facts. He nodded just enough for Boone to see.

"It's bigger than we'd imagined. And filled to the rafters with bombs."

"Bombs?" Christie asked. "I thought they made the gas there."

"They do. They put it in the bombs for delivery."

"So the targets are bombed first, then killed by the gas?"

Boone smiled at her, and there was nothing patronizing in his expression, just affection. "The bombs explode in the air, babe. That's how the gas is deployed."

"Oh." She looked at Tam. "That's why you tested the disbursement system in the cloud chamber. To see if it would spread like the gas. From above."

Nate felt Tam tense under his arm. Her failure to perfect the disbursement still bothered her a lot despite his frequent reassurance that she'd worked miracles with the antidote.

"That's why," she said. "It was supposed to work as effectively as the bombs but…"

"We'll get there," Christie said. "At least, thank God and you, we have an antidote."

"You had no trouble with the fingerprints?" Harper asked.

Nate listened with half an ear as Seth went into detail about getting in and out of the chamber. He wanted to make sure Tam wasn't falling into one of her funks. She tried so hard to hide her depression from him, to make sure he was all right. Still, he worried.

Tam insisted she was fine, but this was her first real experience with failure. She'd told him about her academic career, which had been one success after another. What a hell of a way to miss the mark. The news about the deaths in Chad had made her physically ill.

She put her half finished beer on the ratty carpet, and sunk further into his side. It wasn't possible, not yet, but soon he'd take her back to the room and get her talking. He just hoped she trusted him enough to tell him the truth.

For now, though, he needed to be with the team. A tough road lay ahead and every one of them needed to be heard. No one except Seth had been seriously hurt so far, and Nate intended to keep it that way.

TAM LEFT THE MEETING while Nate was still working out some plans with Vince. She walked around to the back of the motel and stared out at the desert. When she'd first arrived, she'd found it so ugly. But the cactus and the sagebrush had grown on her. Not that she'd want to live here forever, but the view soothed her.

"Hey, you okay?"

She turned, surprised to see that Cade had followed her. Of everyone on the team, she knew the least about him. "Yeah, sure."

He nodded at her, his big muscled arms crossed in front of his burly chest. "I just thought, you know, that maybe what Christie said brought up some bad memories."

She moved closer to him, completely surprised at his observation. He was right, of course, but she'd purposely put on a good show in there. He had to have been focused on her to have picked up on her mood.

"I'm sorry," he said. "I should have kept my mouth shut. I'll go on back and leave you—"

She touched his arm and she heard his sharp inhale. "It's okay. I'm just surprised, that's all. I though I hid it pretty well."

"You did," he said, his gaze moving from her face to her hand and back. "I just, I don't know. I notice things sometimes."

She took her hand away, watching his face. He was a better actor, she thought, than she was. He didn't bat an eyelash. "It must be tough for you here."

"It is for all of us."

"I know. But I heard you left your fiancée when you went to Kosovo."

He nodded.

"I can't imagine."

"I write to her. I don't mail the letters or anything, but I figure when this is over, I'll let her read them."

"She'll appreciate that."

He looked away, toward the distant mountains. "You remind me of her."

"How?"

He shook his head. "It's hard to explain. She's a real nice girl. Loves her family, goes to church. She teaches the fourth grade."

"She sounds great."

"I think so. My friends used to tease me. Said I

should have been born a hundred years ago. But I like that she's simple. Not dumb or anything. She gets a kick out of the simple things, that's all."

"I imagine we'd get along really well."

"I think so."

"You have a picture?"

He reached into his back pocket and brought out a brown leather wallet. His girl's picture was the first thing she saw when he flipped it open. He took the snapshot out and handed it to her.

She was lovely. Long straight dark hair, fresh faced, with a slightly crooked smile. She wouldn't have been considered pretty if it wasn't for her eyes. They were a beautiful blue and they made her look so happy. "What's her name?"

"Ellen."

"She's very pretty. I know you two are going to be so happy."

"She thinks I'm dead."

"I know."

"She's probably got another guy in her life by now."

"Don't think that. Just remember how much she loves you."

"I try."

She wished she had something more positive to say. That she was sure his girl would have waited, but waited for what? For a body? For a miracle?

He took the picture back and put it safely away. "Anyway. Don't worry. You've done fine. Just fine."

"Thank you," she said.

He smiled and walked away toward his single room.

She headed to her room, then straight to the computer. She wanted to dive into work, to pull her weight.

"Hey," Nate said, as he closed the door behind him a moment later.

She booted the computer before she turned to him. "What do you need?"

"You," he said. He sat on the bed and patted the ugly spread. "Here."

"I've got work to do."

"It can wait five minutes."

"Five minutes? Who are you kidding?"

"All right. Ten."

She wanted to say no, but when had she ever been able to turn Nate down? He smiled as she got up, and it occurred to her that Nate was here during the middle of the day instead of downstairs planning with the rest of the team. She sat, but not close enough to touch.

"What's wrong, honey?"

"Are you here because of me? Because of what Christie said?"

"No."

"I don't believe you."

"Okay, fine. I'm here because of you, but not because of what was said."

"Then why?"

"I wanted to be with you. So sue me."

She shook her head. "It's not necessary. Just go on and do what you have to. I'm sure there's something important you're putting off."

"Boone and Seth are sleeping. Cade's working on the plant diagrams. Kate's typing, Vince is complain-

ing. It's all good. I just thought we could have a little
daytime together, that's all."

She didn't really believe him, but he was so damn
charming. When he fell back on the bed, she was too
weak to walk away. She stretched out next to him, which
made her feel small and safe. She loved his size, although
it embarrassed her to admit it. She loved how muscular
he was no matter where she touched him and yet his skin
was surprisingly soft. She even liked the way his chin got
scratchy after a long day, although she wasn't crazy
about the stubble burns she had to deal with later.

He curled himself around her and despite the sun
bleeding through the blinds it felt as if it were night.
When he started rubbing her back, making slow round
circles, she sighed as she visualized all her worries as
balloons floating toward the moon.

"You have to know," he said, his voice as soft as his
touch, "that Christie didn't mean—"

"Nate. Don't sweat it. Cade already talked to me, and
I'm fine."

"Cade?"

"Yes. He was very sweet."

"How sweet?"

She shook her head. "Get your mind out of the gutter."

"Cade?" he asked again, lifting his head from the
pillow.

She put her fingers on his lips, then crawled up his
body and kissed him, making sure he wouldn't speak
again. She wanted nothing more than his comfort and
the amnesia that came with making love.

She could still taste a hint of beer on his tongue,

which was oddly exciting. When he tried to take the lead, she stopped him, thrusting her tongue forcefully. His moan told her he didn't mind all that much, which was good. He didn't have a choice. At least not right now.

It was terribly un-PC of her, but she liked it when he was dominant in bed. Not that he ever made her do anything she didn't want to, but he had taken her right to the edge of her comfort zone a couple of times. She'd never been with a man so strong. Just knowing what he could do if he wanted to made her quiver.

She kept on kissing him as she maneuvered her body over his, straddling his hips. They were so slim compared to his chest, she teased him about being the model for G.I. Joe. He didn't think it was nearly as funny as she did.

His hands went to her waist where he snuck beneath her shirt. It was impossible to be still as his smooth palms caressed her bare skin, so she rubbed her sex over his groin.

Despite her protests he pulled away from her kiss. "Take your clothes off," he said with that gruff voice that made her wet.

She sat up, still straddling him, and stripped off her shirt. Her bra was nothing special, just plain and white, but he always smiled when he saw her in it.

His hands came up and he cupped each breast, squeezing gently, then flicking his thumbs over her covered nipples.

She reached behind and unhooked it, and Nate slipped the straps off her shoulders. God, the way he looked at her. His gaze never moved down, but stayed focused on her face. For a crazy moment, she thought she might cry.

Her hips had stopped moving, but his hadn't. He pushed up, then down, his subtle way of telling her he'd be more comfy with his pants off. She thought about staying right where she was, then decided that was a lose-lose situation.

She dismounted and for the next few minutes it was all about undressing. Once his pants were off, she appreciated his patience. The boy was very hard.

"Come here," he said, lifting her as if she hardly weighed a thing. He put her down on her back with her head on the pillow. His lips came down, but didn't connect. "What do you want?" he whispered.

She spread her legs beneath him. "No bells, no whistles."

"Then I suppose the French maid's uniform is out of the question?"

She bit his lower lip lightly but he yelped anyway.

She laughed, then brought his head back down for a soothing kiss. This time, she didn't stop him from taking her mouth.

His hand slid down her body and when it didn't reach his goal, he twisted until it did. His fingers slid over her lips. He was the one who teased now, dipping in but only for a second. He took his time, even when she lifted her hips.

She supposed the only way to help things along was to offer manual encouragement. She found his hard cock and took one long, slow pull.

He froze, body, fingers, lips.

She smiled and did it again.

That ended the teasing portion of the afternoon.

"Ruthless," he said. "You have no shame."

"None."

"Why is that?"

"Don't know. Must be part of my genetic makeup."

He took her mouth again, then he sat back, slipping out of her grasp. He lifted her legs and put them on his shoulders, then leaned down again, holding himself up with one arm. With his free hand he positioned himself, then he entered her. Not his usual bed-shaking thrust, but slowly. Letting her feel the thickness of his penis as it filled her inch by inch.

When he couldn't go in farther, he stopped. It was an amazing sensation. They were as close as two people could be, and she could feel his pulse down there. Or maybe it was her pulse. Or both.

She closed her eyes, letting herself relax around him, adjusting to her position, and when she felt calm all the way to her toes, she clenched him, using the muscles that counted.

He growled like a animal, but he didn't move. Not yet. He waited until she opened her eyes, and then he pulled slowly out.

"What are you doing to me?" she asked, surprised she sounded breathless.

"This is the no bells, no whistles version," he said. "I want you to know who's inside you."

She closed her eyes at his words, trying not to make this more than it was.

"Don't close your eyes," he said, increasing his pace. "Look at me."

She looked right into his eyes. He kept his head low so there was only inches between them. She could feel his breath on her lips and chin, and see the thickness of his eyelashes.

And while she looked as intently as she ever had, he moved inside her, faster now, shifting the two of them as one on a ride that made the tears come back. She still wasn't sure why, but this time, she wasn't willing to blink. She watched him, rode with him as tears slipped down her cheeks.

His expression changed to one of worry. She just gave him a smile that told him she was fine. He didn't nod because that would have broken the trance.

She was grateful now for the light coming through the blinds. Grateful that she had him, terrified it could all be gone in a blink.

She felt him tremble, saw how hard it was for him to keep his silent promise. His lower half was taking over, and she gave in gracefully. He didn't need to prove a thing.

When his eyes closed, she reached between them to his small nipples. She took each one between finger and thumb and she grasped him with more force than she would have been able to take. But he did. His head reared back, and he slammed into her, seconds from his climax.

Releasing him, she flicked the nipples with her thumbnails, moving faster as he got closer.

His mouth opened, his face contorted, and he was

there. He didn't thrust again, but he pressed against her as if he needed to get closer still.

She loved the way he came. He grunted and his cheeks turned a dull red, but it was unashamed and so close to the bone that she felt incredibly connected.

It was doubly interesting, because she hadn't come. He usually made sure she did, even before he entered her. But this time, no. It was fine. He'd given her exactly what she wanted. She felt amazingly satisfied even after he'd rolled to her side.

"I'll get up in a minute," he said, panting as if he'd won a marathon.

She kissed his shoulder. "Don't move." She got out of bed and went to the bathroom. On her way, she realized something else. They hadn't used a condom.

She wondered if she'd get pregnant, and how she'd feel about that. By the time she closed the bathroom door, she'd decided she didn't know, and didn't much care.

NATE WOKE WITH A START at the knock on the door, and his weapon was in his hand before he realized it was already dark. He looked at Tam who was sitting up, drawing the covers over her naked breasts.

He didn't give a damn about being naked himself. He got up, went to the door and looked through the peephole. Then he pulled the blinds back a little and saw that it was Harper and she was alone.

"Hold on a minute," he said.

She nodded.

He smiled at Tam's blinking confusion as he put

away his gun. "It's Harper. She'll wait while we get decent."

"I'm always decent," she said. "And sometimes I'm naked."

He laughed as he yanked his jeans on and then his T-shirt, purposely keeping his eyes off Tam. Even when he should know better, looking at her in the buff made him crazy.

He wasn't at all sure what had happened this afternoon. He hadn't come that hard since that first time with her. She hadn't come at all. What the hell?

"Why are you just standing there?"

He snapped out of his minifugue at Tam's urgent whisper. "You ready?"

"Yes. Go let her in."

The moment he opened the door, he knew something had happened. He pulled Harper in and before the door was shut he said, "What's wrong?"

Harper looked at Tam, then at the floor. "I hope we're wrong."

Tam joined him, and he put his arm around her shoulder. Harper looked at her again, but this time, she didn't turn away. "We saw it on the news. I wasn't sure, but Kate said—"

"Damn it, Harper," Nate said, his anger rising along with his fear. "What the hell is going on?"

"Tam, your parents are Joseph and Lorraine?"

Instantly, Tam was trembling, her whole body, as if she'd been plugged into a current. "Why?"

"They've been injured."

Tam looked up at him with wide, terrified eyes. It

was just like the night he'd found her crouching in the dark, maybe worse.

Without turning away, he spoke to Harper. "Injured how?"

"There was an explosion at their house."

Tam's eyes closed as her lips parted. She didn't weigh much, so he was able to keep her standing with just the one arm.

"Are they alive?" he asked.

"They're both in critical condition. I wrote down the hospital name in case you wanted it."

Tam's hand went out to get the small piece of paper. He could feel her horror, her fear, her helplessness. And still, he put his hand over hers and brought it to her side.

This time, he wasn't able to hold her.

# *10*

TAM WAS IN CHRISTIE AND BOONE's room, but she couldn't remember how she got there. The whole team was there, all of them whispering as if she were sick, as if she was the one in the hospital.

Nate sat next to her, but when he tried to touch her, she flinched. She didn't want his comfort or his explanations. She wanted to go home.

"Tam?" Kate stood in front of her with a mug in her hand. "I made you some tea."

She didn't want it, but she was too exhausted to explain, so she took it and put it on the side table. It was habit that made her say, "Thanks," not gratitude.

She hated these people. Every last one of them. They had no idea what it was like not knowing if her parents were alive or dead. To know they'd been injured because of her.

"Isn't there some way…?" Christie asked.

"I've been thinking about that," Seth said. "Maybe we could get a message to one of the hospital administrators. Tell them that Tam is undercover—"

"You don't think they've thought of that?" Nate asked. "They've thought of everything, and if they get so much as a hint that Tam is trying to make contact…"

"She has to know how they are," Christie said, her voice sharp and angry. "It's not right."

Nate looked at his sister with grave eyes. "It can't be done. Not yet. We'll get through this, and then she'll be free to go see them. Even then she'll have to be careful. Her parents believe she's dead."

"If it were Mom—"

"We'd do the same thing. Christie, it'll only be worse for them if Omicron thinks they know something. It's just good it was on the news. Made public. Now that they're in the hospital—"

"I'm right here," Tam said, stopping the futile conversation. "I know I can't call them, okay? I know they might already be dead, and I can't do a thing. I know all that, can't you please stop talking about it?"

The room got quiet and, perversely, that made things even worse. She wanted to walk, to run, to do anything except sit in this filthy motel. She was a scientist. And a fool. She'd been duped. Lied to. By everyone.

"We're so close, Tam." Nate's voice was calm, and it made her want to scream. "A few days, that's all."

"They could be dead by then."

"So could a lot of other people."

"I don't care," she said. "About any of it."

"I know," he whispered. "They're counting on that. They're trying to break you."

She stood up, surprising Nate. "They've succeeded, okay? They've won. I give up." She turned around, glaring at whoever looked her way, then up to the microphones she prayed were in the walls, to the satellites spinning above the earth. "I give up," she screamed, as loudly as she could. "Just stop it, please." Her tears blinded her and her knees grew weak, but she needed them to hear. "Please!"

She covered her face and wept. She wanted her momma, her papa. She wanted to go back in time, to throw the recruiter out on his ass, she wanted—

A hand held her arm, and then she felt a sharp pinch in her shoulder. It was Harper with a needle. She jerked away. "What—"

"It's a sedative. You'll sleep."

"Damn it. I don't want to sleep."

"I'm sorry," Harper said, and Tam saw that tears were running down her face, too.

Nate came to her side, trying once more to hold her.

"Don't," she said, twisting away. "Leave me alone. None of you understand."

Nate just nodded. "It's okay. I won't touch you. I won't make you do anything you don't want to."

She slapped him across the face. She hadn't meant to, and instantly she wanted to take it back.

He didn't even move. Not a flinch, not a blink. He just kept looking at her with tortured eyes.

That was it, all she could take. Everything was wrong, and it was all her fault.

Then she was on the ground, but she couldn't remember how she got there.

"I HATE TO LEAVE LIKE this," Seth said, keeping his voice low. Tam was passed out in Boone's bed, but no one knew for how long, or how bad it would be when she woke up.

"I know," Harper said. She kissed him, then kissed him again. "We have to finish this. God knows I don't want you to go into that place again. But it has to end. None of us can go on like this much longer."

He nodded, then looked past her to the closed bedroom door. "I thought it was bad enough that I couldn't call home. My parents are fine."

Harper didn't know what to say. She just wanted him safe. If she lost him…

"All right," he said, his voice firm and strong. Her soldier was back. "It's time to lock and load. You be good and take care of them, okay?"

She nodded. "I'll do my best."

After one last kiss he headed out the door, followed closely by Boone and Cade. The men weren't going into the chamber tonight, but they would still be in danger. They had to map the outside of the plant, to find all the electrical outlets, vents, phone lines. It would take them till just before dawn, as usual, but tonight, Harper knew, would crawl by. There would be no sleep. Not until they came back home.

Harper watched them until the truck disappeared, then she closed the door. Vince held Kate on the couch. Christie sat on the floor by the bedroom door. Nate was inside with Tam, but he'd honored his words. He had taken the chair with him, and if she knew Nate, he wouldn't budge until Tam was awake.

Harper stared blindly at that warped door, wondering why she'd cried when she gave Tam the shot. It was so unlike her.

Harper had no relationship at all with her parents. She didn't miss them because they'd been gone since she was a kid. Her father in prison, her mother married to a man who had money, neither giving her a second thought.

It was better this way. She might have missed out on some of the good stuff, but she'd never go through Tam's version of hell.

She went to the kitchen and poured herself a cup of coffee. As she sipped, she figured she'd better check her medical kit again. Tam might wake up mellow, but Harper doubted it.

She took her cup and sat down on the floor, her black bag in front of her. Just then the bedroom door flew open, but it wasn't Tam. It was Nate, and from the look on his face, something bad had gone down. Real bad.

He walked past her, past everyone, to the door, and then he was gone.

She looked at Christie, who seemed damned scared. Vince stood up, but he didn't make a move until Kate pulled him back down to the couch.

Harper got out another vial of sedative and filled a new needle. She hoped her supply lasted through the night. She turned to Christie. "Go in with her. See what you can do. I'll be back."

She went outside, but she didn't have to go far to find Nate. He was in the parking lot, standing very still. She closed the door quietly and waited.

The explosion came quickly. He kicked the tire of Vince's truck, banged his fist on the window. It clearly wasn't enough. He kicked the door, said a few choice curses so loudly it scared her and then he reached behind his back and drew his weapon.

"Nate! Stop!"

He turned, but he had enough sense not to point the gun at her. "Go back inside, Harper."

"Not a chance."

"I'm warning you—"

"What? You're going to shoot me? Shoot up the motel?"

He stared at her for a long minute, the single street lamp painting him in shadow. "I can't do this."

She took a measured step toward him. "Can't do what?"

"I can't save everyone."

"You don't have to."

His face broke, but only for a moment. He got himself together again as she moved closer. "I can't save her."

The words had been spoken softly, but they hit harder than his shout. "It's not your fault, Nate."

"You think that's a comfort?"

"No. I'm a doctor, remember? I've had a lot of time to wish I could save the world. We can only do our best."

"My best is bullshit. She won't even look at me. I should have let her call her parents."

"You think it would be better if she led Omicron here? Remember, they're the bad guys, Nate. Leland Ingram. Senator Raines." She was right in front of him now, and she wished he'd put the damn gun away. "The only thing that's kept us alive is that we've stuck together. We all need you, Nate, not just Tam. We need her, too. And Seth, and Boone, and all the others. Hell, we even need me. So get this out of your system. Go beat up the truck again. Howl at the moon. But then you have to come back, you hear me?"

It hurt to look at him, his pain was so raw. She'd had no idea it was so serious between the two of them. That would have been great news if Tam's parents hadn't been targeted. God, the choice he'd had to make. Give the woman he loved the chance to speak to her dying parents, or complete the mission. It must have killed him to stop her from taking the phone number.

"I don't know what to do," he said.

That had to have been a painful admission. Nate Pratchett was a leader. To show weakness was worse even than death.

"The best thing you can do for Tam is to finish this. We have to expose them. We have to win."

He looked away, bringing his face into the light. She watched as he made his decision. His jaw muscle flexed, his lips pressed together. He got back his mojo right there in front of her.

She didn't know how it would end with him and Tam, but the only chance they all had was to fight. When the dust settled, they'd find out who they were apart and together. Before she'd fallen for Seth, she'd have given them one chance in a million. Now? She wanted them to win, too.

THERE WERE MORE GUARDS on patrol at the plant than usual. Seth wondered if they were getting ready to ship out the armaments. It wouldn't surprise him. The chamber had been ninety percent full.

He looked to his right, at Boone and Cade as they crawled under the fence at the eastern perimeter. Once through, they'd have seven minutes to make it to the rear of the processing plant. They'd split up then and go quadrant by quadrant, mapping the exterior, paying special attention to any points of egress or entrance.

They also needed to see inside one particular window. From the inside of the chamber, they'd sighted a sterile room that was fully self-contained. Inside were the computers and the operators who ran the chamber. None of the personnel had worn chem suits, which told them a lot about the structure of the room itself.

It was also clear that there was a separate entrance. One personnel could access from the outside.

Their aim tonight would be to find a way to get in that room.

He crawled forward, using his claw to propel him in ways his other hand couldn't. He'd learned how to do almost everything he needed to with the claw. It was still a pain, but at least he wasn't helpless.

Once he reached the inside of the fence, he turned back to make sure there were no signs of a cut in the wire. They'd rigged it so that the electrical feed that monitored the fence for breaches had been traversed, so no alarms would give them away.

He hit the dirt with only seconds to spare as a jeep with two MPs rolled by about a hundred feet from where he hid.

He knew Boone and Cade were doing likewise,

checking their watches carefully to know when to hide and when to work.

Even though they'd done this time and again, there was no getting used to it. No way to relax, not for a moment.

It was time. He rose, adjusted his infrared glasses and started toward the plant.

TAM DRIFTED IN AND OUT OF consciousness. She imagined the worst for her parents and when that became unbearable she took refuge in her anger.

Nate had promised to keep her safe. He'd promised to take her out of this nightmare. The bastard had given her hope.

Her naiveté had cost her everything. Her reputation, her safety, her future. What did she have to look forward to? Even if they did get out of this, no one would hire her. She'd helped Omicron develop the gas. It didn't matter that she hadn't known what her part in the process had been for. That only made things worse. And no one would care that she'd come up with the antidote.

By the time this thing was over—if she wasn't dead—every scientist and research facility in the world would know of her duplicity.

Ignoring Christie, who'd taken Nate's place in the chair by the wall, she turned over, wanting nothing more than to sleep. If she could just still her thoughts, her exhaustion would take over. Maybe it would be better to just ask Harper for another shot.

So, she wasn't finished typing in all her notes. She didn't care.

The image of her mother came to her, only she was covered in bandages, connected to tubes and monitors. It was so vivid, she couldn't stop the low moan that wanted to be a scream.

A second later, Christie was by her side, and she touched Tam's arm, but she didn't jerk away. She had no energy at all, not even enough to chase Nate's sister out of the room.

"Tam, let me get you something to drink. Your throat must be parched."

It was. Every part of her felt parched, as if she'd been baking in the desert. She closed her eyes.

Sometime later, she woke to a fuzzy darkness. Disoriented, she reached over to see if Nate was with her, but his side was empty. She wondered what time it was, and if she could shower before he came home. Then she remembered.

Her parents were still in the hospital or worse. Nate was not a superhero. She was still alone. Pain shot through her body as she brought her knees up toward her chin.

"There's water next to you."

Her eyes opened at the sound of Nate's voice. Christie had been here. Tam had told Nate to go to hell and stay there. Or had she dreamed all that?

With a shaky hand, she reached for the plastic glass and rose to her elbow to drink. The cool water felt amazingly good. She didn't even care that she spilled.

When she had enough, she put the glass back. She had to go to the bathroom, a Herculean task. But she sat up, put her legs on the floor. Rested a minute, then stood.

She fully expected Nate to come to her rescue, and she planned to tell him once again where he could go, but he didn't make a move. When she passed him, he didn't even look at her. He just sat very still on a chair that was too small.

When she closed the bathroom door, she rested her forehead on the wood. It was too much. All of it.

IT WAS AFTER 6:00 a.m. and Christie was going to lose it if Boone didn't get home soon. They'd never been this late. The knots in her stomach told her something had gone wrong.

She went into the kitchen to make another pot of coffee. Between her, Harper, Kate, Vince and Nate, they'd finished off so many pots they'd have to buy more when the store opened. She felt queasy from all the caffeine, but that wasn't enough to stop her from having another cup.

Harper had switched to tea a few hours ago, but she was just as anxious. It was their men out there. If something had gone wrong, how would they know?

The guys wouldn't come home, yes, but would that mean they were dead? Captured? In prison?

Christie's hand shook as she counted out the spoons. She spilled water all over the counter, but screw it, she didn't care.

All she could think of was Boone. He'd saved her. Before he'd come into her life, she'd known nothing about Omicron and believed that her brother was dead. Then the stalker had taken over her life. It was Boone who'd come to the rescue. He'd trapped the stalker, and that's when she'd found out what a long reach Omicron had. They had been behind the stalking. They'd taken her job, her home, all her money. It was the worst thing she'd ever experienced. If it hadn't been for Boone…

He'd been kind and strong and she loved him with all her heart. Only the discovery that Nate was alive had been as sweet.

Kate joined her in the kitchen. "Give them time," she said. "They had so much to do."

Christie smiled, but she knew if it had been Vince out there, Kate wouldn't be so calm. She turned back to watch the coffee brew, hugging her middle as if it would help. Nothing would help but the truck pulling into the parking lot. She had to see him, to know that he was alive and not hurt. They'd gone too far for it to fall apart now. They'd fought impossible odds, and still they were all here.

She'd never hated anything the way she hated Omicron. They should all burn in hell, every last one of—

"The truck."

It was Harper. She'd already opened the front door and was standing outside. Christie ran to join her, and so did Kate, Vince and Nate.

The truck stopped and there was Boone. He wasn't bloody, he had all his limbs. But he looked like hell. Seth got out of the passenger side. If anything, he looked worse than Boone.

Her eyes went to the back of the truck, waiting to see if Cade had been hurt. But Cade wasn't there.

# *11*

NATE FELT AS THOUGH HE'D been gut shot. Cade had been taken, either by Omicron's men or a bullet. Either way, he wasn't coming back.

It was getting too light outside for them to stand here in the parking lot, so he ushered them inside.

He headed straight to the bedroom to check on Tam. She was on her side, curled up, and if he hadn't known her so well, he'd have thought she was sleeping.

He couldn't deal with her right now. It killed him to see her like this, but his friend was gone and there were things that had to be done.

He left the door open, hoping Tam would hear the conversation. He wasn't sure what he wanted from her, except to let him in.

Seth and Boone were on the couch. Kate and Vince had taken the far corner, Harper and Christie sat on the floor, touching the guys. They were all in the debrief position and it was up to him to ask the questions.

"What happened?"

Seth and Boone looked at each other, then quickly away. They'd left a man behind, and that was not okay for two soldiers like them.

"He's dead," Boone said. He opened his mouth again, but he couldn't seem to speak.

It was Seth who looked at Nate now. "We were on our way out. Something caught his uniform, and when the guards came by, they spotted him. He started yelling so we could get away."

"We tried to get back to him but the guards were right there. They called in reinforcements and they weren't backing down. There was no way we were going to get him out of there," Boone said.

"And we had to get back with the intel." Seth's head dropped and his shoulders shook. Nate wanted to cry, too. He'd really liked the guy. They'd had some good times overseas, and while Cade hadn't been much for the bars, he enjoyed hearing the men's stories.

"When they pulled him out from under the fence, he put up a struggle, but it was just to get more men around him."

Nate could see how hard Boone was holding onto Christie's hand. To her credit, she didn't even wince.

"The grenade did maximum damage, both in personnel and obfuscation."

"What?" Kate asked. "What does that mean?"

Nate turned. "It means that Cade blew himself up, along with those men around him. He left minimal evidence, so they would find it difficult to identify him."

"He blew himself—" She turned away, and Vince pulled her into his arms.

"It's what he had to do," Nate said, hoping like hell his voice wouldn't give him away. "Boone or Seth would have done the same. The objective is to keep our presence here a secret."

"You would have done that?" Christie asked, looking up at Boone. "Without even telling me that was the plan?"

Boone looked guilty, but he nodded. "I didn't want you to worry any more than you had to. I'm sorry, but it's the risk we take."

Tears ran down her cheeks, but she didn't argue with him. Harper had wrapped her arm around Seth's leg, and his hand was on her shoulder.

"What now?" Vince asked quietly.

"We assume Omicron's been alerted to our presence. Pack everything, even the trash. We leave here at night-fall."

"Where are we going?"

"There's an abandoned apartment building about twenty miles north of here. We'll stay there. Vince, you need to get all the cash from the bank. Kate, get with Eli, tell him we're a go the day after tomorrow. Remember, nothing gets left behind."

"I haven't finished."

The voice startled him, and Nate turned to the bedroom door. Tam was leaning on the wall looking pale and shaky. "You haven't finished what?" he asked, and even he noticed the change in his own demeanor. From a commander to a concerned lover in a heartbeat.

"I haven't finished my assignment. The notes aren't ready."

"I'll pack your gear," he said, wanting more than anything on earth to take her away from all this. To keep her safe. But he couldn't make anyone safe. Soldiers, civilians, women, kids. All he could do was fight.

"I'll get started," she said, heading toward the door. She had to pass him closely, there was no other choice. But she didn't look at him, and he didn't try to touch her.

"Did he have family?" Kate asked.

Nate's gaze had followed Tam, and the question stopped her with her hand on the knob.

"Cade's parents live in Idaho. He has an older brother and a younger sister, and he left behind his college sweetheart. Her name is Ellen."

"They were engaged," Tam said. "He wrote to her, every night, even though he couldn't mail the letters." She went outside. Nate watched until the door closed behind her.

SHE FELT HEARTSICK. Tam felt so weary she could barely walk to her room. She'd liked Cade. He'd been quiet and sweet, and damn it, she'd had a strong suspicion he'd had a little crush on her since the day they'd met, despite his love for Ellen. It was easy to see he'd been raised by an old-fashioned family.

They were right around the same age, but he couldn't help calling her ma'am. Or maybe that had been the soldier in him. She'd never know.

She made it inside her room and her gaze went straight to the bed. The sheets and pillows were still messed up from when she'd had sex with Nate. The realization that she'd been in bed with him while her parents' house had exploded around them had come to her earlier, and now she could add Cade's death to the picture.

God, she couldn't think about that if she expected to get anything done. She went to the computer, turned it on and then grabbed her notebook from under the table.

Her life might have fallen apart, but she still had a life and she owed it to Cade to get busy. Tam couldn't imagine the strength it had taken to pull that pin on the grenade. It was unimaginable, and yet as she'd listened to Boone and Seth relate how he had died, the truth of her situation hit her.

Her parents were injured because of the evil men behind Omicron. Men who thought innocent lives were as disposable as garbage. Men whose self-righteousness made them a threat to anyone in their way. Seth's hand. Cade's life. Her parents. They were nothing to those men. They'd wiped out whole villages. What was one soldier? Or a couple mourning what they assumed was the death of their daughter?

She didn't know what the body count was but if she had anything to do with it, it wouldn't get any higher.

She double-clicked on the program she needed to finish her work. There was a lot more to do, and no matter what, she would get it done right.

Ten minutes after she began typing, Nate walked in. He didn't speak to her, but she could feel his presence as he took out his duffel bag and began to pack.

Her anger had ebbed and she could admit to herself that he hadn't really lied to her. She'd felt safe with him because it was easier than facing the truth. He'd let her because he needed someone who believed he could do anything he set his mind to.

They'd both been willing participants, and it wasn't fair to make him the bad guy. But it also wasn't fair to make him the hero, either.

Nate was a terrific leader, there was no doubt about that. She didn't know squat about being a soldier, but she knew he was as good as it got. Still, he was human. His troops were miniscule, his resources laughable. He was doing the best he could under the circumstances, but he wasn't magician.

She understood now why Seth had come to talk to her about Nate. He'd seen her hero-worship and he'd worried about the inevitable crash once she pushed Nate from his pedestal. He'd been right to be concerned.

She should apologize for being so hurtful before, but neither of them could afford to be distracted. She had to transcribe. He had to pack. They had to win.

Later, when they were somewhere else, somewhere they'd never made love, she'd tell him.

THEY'D COME TO HIM, two at a time, to say they wanted one more day. That even if Omicron realized it was Cade who'd died, and therefore the rest of them must be nearby, Omicron wasn't going to find the motel that night. They wanted to mourn, think, rest, eat, type.

Nate knew exactly what they wanted to do. They wanted to screw each other to oblivion. Kate and Vince, Christie and Boone, Harper and Seth, because, damn it, they were alive, and they might not be tomorrow.

He knew because he wanted Tam in a way that unnerved him. That made him stand at the back of his room and stare at her for a good ten minutes. All she did was type. She transcribed her notes without looking up. She wasn't thinking about him at all.

That realization chased him out of his room, down the stairs with the duffel bag and his backpack. He'd gone to Cade's room and that's where the others had found him. By the time Kate and Vince had been assured of their one night reprieve, Nate was wiped out.

It hurt that he had to pack for his friend. That there was no body to bury. It hurt so much because Cade had died on Nate's watch. He'd been so busy with Tam he'd taken his eyes off the prize.

He should have been the one out there with Boone and Seth. He should have been in better communication with his men. The plan had inherent flaws, but he was too close to see them. He'd get them all killed. And who the hell was Leland Ingram to bomb Tam's parents' home, and what made Senator Jackson Raines think he deserved to live another second when a good man like Cade Huston was dead?

A searing pain shot through Nate's hand and he looked down to see blood dripping on the filthy bathroom floor. He looked around, but there was no one there, and then he saw he'd cut himself on a safety razor. Cade's razor.

He threw the thing in the sink and hissed as he washed out the small but deep cut in his palm. He took one of the towels off the rack and wrapped his hand, then he left the bathroom to sit on Cade's unmade bed.

They'd gotten him a single room. No kitchen, no couch. Just an old bed and a TV that didn't get but three channels. He'd laughed about it, said he wasn't likely to get lucky in Nevada, and that had been it. He'd eaten dinner at Christie's. He'd taken care of the weapons. He'd written to his girl every single night.

He'd killed himself to protect his friends.

The American people would know the truth about him. His family would learn he was a hero and they'd be proud. Nate would make sure of that.

A wave of exhaustion hit him so hard he felt sick to his stomach. He laid back on the bed, the scent of Cade's god awful aftershave all over the sheets.

To his shame, his last thoughts were of Tam, not his fallen comrade.

"TAM?"

With a gasp, Tam looked up at Kate, standing inside the room, holding a plate. "Oh, God, you scared me."

"I'm sorry to come in like this, but I knocked and—"

"No, no, it's my fault." Tam glanced at the window and saw it was dark, then she looked at the time stamp on her computer. Ten past ten. Jeez. "Are we supposed to go now?"

"Nate didn't tell you? We're staying until tomorrow."

"No, he didn't."

Kate nodded, her long dark hair striking against her white sweater. "Have you eaten anything?"

Tam shook her head, but she was more concerned with the loss of time than hunger. "I know this is a dumb question, but did all this happen today?"

"Last night and today," Kate said softly. She came over to the table and put the plate down. It was a big ham and cheese sandwich with lettuce and tomato, along with a bag of chips and some carrot and celery sticks.

The sight of it made Tam's stomach growl so loudly Kate raised her eyebrows. "I think you'd better eat."

"Thanks," she said. "I'm trying to finish this up, but I'm not that great at typing numbers. I have to look at the keyboard."

Kate went to the bed and sat down. "Me too, and I'm an accountant, remember?"

Tam took a bite out of the sandwich. It was amazingly good. She took another, and a third before she spoke. "I know I was horrible. I'm sorry."

Kate shrugged. "You weren't so bad. It's horrible that you can't go see the people you love."

"You miss your family, don't you?"

"Me? Yeah. All the time. Every day. My father has a heart condition, and I'm not even sure he's alive."

"Shit."

Kate dipped her head, then look up at Tam. "Nate's doing his best, you know."

Tam's cheeks heated. "I know."

"Okay. I just thought—"

"That I was being unfair. Nate's been great to me. He's saved my sanity and my life."

"But?"

"It was a mistake to share this room."

"Was it?"

Tam put her sandwich down. "It wasn't fair to either of us. Too much going on. Too much riding on things outside of our control."

"People don't fall in love on schedule. It doesn't matter what's happening out in the world."

"I don't know if I agree."

Kate smiled. "It's okay. I'm prejudiced. I had no business falling in love with Vince. He had no business leaving his life to join our motley crew. But I'm glad we did."

"I don't love Nate."

"No?"

"At least, I don't think so. I don't know. He was virtually my only contact for over two years. When you guys thought he was dead, he was making sure I was all right, that I had food and equipment. He was my lifeline. He still is. How can I tell if it's love?"

"I don't have any answers for you. All I know is that we all need Nate to be one hundred percent. He needs to be focused on the mission, for everyone's sake."

"What are you saying. You want me to sleep with him?"

"That's up to you. Look, I like you, Tam, I have since we met in Kosovo. I'm really sorry about your parents, believe me."

Tam closed her eyes. "But I'm not leading the troops into battle."

Kate stood. "Nate lost a member of his team today. And he's lost you."

"I understand."

"You better finish that," Kate said, nodding toward the plate of food. Then she headed for the door. Just before she left, she said, "He's down in Cade's room."

# *12*

NATE STUDIED THE DRAWINGS of the plant, this time concentrating only on communications. It was right there, the exit door that connected the clean room to the outside, that would make or break the entire plan.

His eyes blurred but this time blinking didn't clear his vision. He gathered the diagrams strewn over what used to be Cade's bed and sat down, knowing he had to sleep, wondering if he dared go back to his room.

Was she in bed? If he tried to join her, would she turn away?

All of this was his fault. He'd never let himself get emotionally involved on a mission. That was the kiss of death, and he'd known that since basic training. Afterwards, that's when fraternizing was all right. Women were great to celebrate with, and even better when a man needed to lick his wounds. Women were distractions. Not all women, of course. But a woman like Tam? He knew better.

Hadn't he told himself she was off limits? Every time he'd gone into her lab, he'd wanted her, sure, but he was a man of discipline. Restraint. Right up until the moment she'd crooked her little finger, and then he folded like a pair of deuces.

Now it was crunch time, only days away from the end game, and was he thinking about timing, coordination, weapons? No. He was thinking about never touching her again. Never seeing her eyes light up with mischief and pleasure when she tried some new trick in bed.

He wanted her, and it hurt like hell that she didn't want him back. His past conquests must be feeling pretty smug about now. Who'd it been, Reiko? No, it had been Illana who'd told him that one day he'd fall, and fall hard. That he'd be the biggest fool of them all.

Piss-poor time to learn that lesson, when his life could be measured in hours. He needed to get some sleep and make sure that the one and only thing on his mind was the mission.

They each had a vital part to play in the next few days, but as in every ensemble piece, they needed a steady conductor.

After it was over, he'd make it up to her. For now, if he didn't sleep he wouldn't be good for anything. He set his wristwatch alarm for 6:00 a.m. That would give him a good four hours of rest.

He settled himself on the bed, and forced himself to stop thinking about Tam. About Cade. About anything at all.

IT WAS JUST PAST 2:00 a.m. and Tam still couldn't decide. She'd walked along, gun in hand, and she'd stood in front of Cade's door until the cold permeated her shoes, her pants, even her jacket. She'd raised her hand to knock at least four times, but she couldn't go through with it.

The light underneath the door told her he was still

awake. He shouldn't be. Maybe Kate was right. Maybe the best thing she could do to support the mission was sleep with Nate. Make sure he ate, that he got some rest.

If it was only sleep, she'd be able to handle it. But it wouldn't be. She would turn to him for comfort, because that's what she did. He would touch her and she doubted she'd say no. What she needed was time. And just a little bit of normalcy. Even more than that, she wanted her mother. To talk to her, get her advice. To know that she was okay, and that Papa was okay.

She knocked on the door, then wiped her eyes with the edge of her jacket.

Nate opened it a few seconds later, gun in hand. "What's wrong?"

"I woke you."

He blinked as if he hadn't realized it was her. "Tam. What time is it?"

"Two."

He looked behind her at the parking lot, then stepped back. "Come in."

She hesitated, but the damage had been done. He was awake now, and knowing Nate, he wouldn't fall back into bed.

He closed the door, engaged the safety on his gun, but he didn't relax or move. "Did something happen?"

"I've finished," she said. "All my notes are compiled and ready."

"That's good. I think Kate might need some help finishing hers. I'd like to have them done by tomorrow."

"I'll get on that." She could barely look at him. Embarrassment over her behavior, confusion about what she felt, those were minor compared to how very much she wanted to be held in his strong arms. She yearned for that feeling of safety only he could give, even though she knew it was a complete illusion.

"I was just going over the plant diagrams—"

"You were sleeping, and I woke you. I'm sorry. I saw the light on, and I—"

"It's all right. I just thought I'd catch a few hours before we have to get moving." He looked at the bed, then crossed his arms over his chest, mirroring the way she'd been standing since she walked in.

"Nate, I'm sorry."

"For what?" he asked, too quickly.

"You know what for. I was very upset and I said things I shouldn't have."

"You didn't say anything wrong."

She let her arms drop to her side. "I said plenty. Maybe not in words, but you got the message. You've done nothing wrong. Been nothing but good to me."

He took a step toward her. "I'm so sorry about your parents."

"I know. And I know if it was possible, you would've seen to it that I got to them. But it's not. You were right to stop me."

"I—" He stopped. "It's late. We both should get some sleep."

"Come back to the room with me."

"Do you think that's a good idea?"

"Not a clue. But I don't think you should sleep here."

He winced at the reminder that his friend was gone. "Yeah. I'll get my things."

She went to the bed and put all the papers together in a neat stack as he got his duffel bag, and Cade's. She carried Nate's backpack and she straightened the bed before they left.

Back in their room, she saw he'd left her toothbrush and paste and her soap and hair things. He'd left the awful Goodwill nightgown and what she'd need for the morning. Everything he owned was in his duffel bag. Yet another reason to feel lousy.

He didn't make a big deal out of it. They got ready for bed as if nothing had happened, but when she found herself lying next to him in the dark, she knew it was a very big deal. Maybe not for Nate. He wasn't much older than she was, but he was years ahead of her in worldliness.

She felt like a teenager, and in a lot of ways she was. Her nose had been stuck in a book, and her eyes at a microscope for most of her life. She knew exactly nothing about men, especially not one as complex as Nate.

"Are you okay?" he asked.

She laughed. "I'm the opposite of okay."

"What can I do?"

"You can get some rest. You have to be sharp, and I'll feel even worse if you stay awake because of me."

He lay so still for so long, she thought he'd taken her advice. She was about to turn over and close her own eyes when he said, "I want to hold you."

Simple words spoken so softly, yet they tore her up. Tears burned in her tired eyes, her hands fisted and she could hardly breathe.

"Forget it," he said. "I'm—"

She reached out with her hand and touched his arm. "I want to be held."

He moved slowly, inching toward to her until she felt his thigh, his hip, his shoulder. Then he slipped his arm under her neck. When he pulled her closer, she gave up the fight. It was most likely the worst thing she could do, and she'd regret it for the rest of her life, but she'd never been more grateful for the comfort and safety she felt cradled beside him. He wasn't a wizard or a superhero, but he came closer than anyone she'd ever known.

With her hand on his chest, she tenderly kissed his cheek, and they slept.

THE MORNING BEGAN WITH A meeting in Christie's room. Nate had slept until six, and he wouldn't have gotten up then if Tam hadn't been crying.

She hadn't even been awake. He could guess what her nightmare was about, but she didn't say, and he wasn't sure he should ask.

He knew she wasn't sure about this, about them being together, and he wasn't either. But he was grateful for the truce. Maybe they'd never figure out what they should be doing, but in the meantime, he felt a whole hell of a lot better with Tam by his side.

She was pale and shaky as she sat next to him on Christie's couch, but when he looked at her, she managed a smile.

He turned to the troops. "Vince, you have everything we'll need?"

"Not everything," he said. He must have just rolled

out of bed. His hair was all over the place, he hadn't shaved and his shirt wasn't buttoned right. Kate, on the other hand, looked great, and the way she smiled at Vince was pure indulgence. "I've got to get to Mesquite again, and I'm picking up the canisters at the machine shop."

Nate nodded. "I assume everyone's packed?"

"What about the computers?" Kate asked. "I'm not finished with mine. Are we taking them?"

"Yes, we are. And Tam will help you with the transcription."

"Okay, boss."

"I've got to make some phone calls," Harper said. "Will we get reception at the new digs?"

"I have no idea. We'll try, and if not, we'll find the nearest cell tower."

"What about Eli?" Seth asked.

"He said it's all a go, but I want you to run through all the electronics again. You and Boone, as soon as we're over there."

"Wait," Christie said. "I have to take Milo to the vet. I can't just leave him on his own."

"Okay," Nate said. "You take him in, but get back as soon as you can."

She nodded.

"Right people." Nate put his coffee cup down on the carpet. "We're leaving in shifts, two at a time in half hour intervals."

Tam and Nate were the last to go. The ride wasn't long, and it was quiet, but it wasn't tense. Mostly because Nate was in command mode, which is exactly where he needed to be.

She kept herself on the far side of the passenger seat, low and silent. Nate looked over several times, but she just smiled to let him know all was well.

It wasn't, of course, but she wasn't about to tell him. She hadn't been able to shake her nightmare. She'd been at the hospital, in the room with her parents. Just as she touched her mother's arm, the alarms went off. Her mother coded and Tam was pushed out of the way as doctors and nurses tried to revive her. No one turned off the heart monitor, and she listened to her mother's death. Then Nate had shaken her awake.

Tam wasn't a superstitious person, but something told her it hadn't all been a dream. Her mother was gone.

"There it is."

She stared ahead at what could only be called a ghost town. There were some abandoned shacks on the sides of the road, and a bar with broken and boarded windows. An old grocery store, some more houses and behind a gas station that hadn't had a customer in years was a two-story apartment building that had one window upstairs that wasn't broken. "It's not bad."

"At least it's not summer. This place would be an oven." Nate turned onto another pitted road while she stared at her new residence. She didn't see any sign of the others, which was good. That meant Omicron wouldn't see them, either.

The truck slowed as Nate reached the far end of the building. Behind it was a parking area. None of the other trucks were there, either. "Where is everyone?"

"Indoor parking," he said.

She saw what he meant. The back half of the building on the right side was open, but the roof and second floor were still intact. All the trucks were there. They'd be invisible from a helicopter. "Smart."

"Yep." He pulled carefully into the last possible space, and when she got out, the others were there to greet them.

Carrying several bags, she was led into the inner rooms. The place had been swept, but there was still dust everywhere. Without windows, the rooms were cold as hell, but there was a fire pit, and a couple of camp stoves in the remains of an old kitchen. "Vince got all this?"

Nate nodded. "There's more."

She followed him to what used to be someone's living room where there were three tables, all of them pretty big, with mismatched chairs. On one of the tables were two computers, both of which were connected to a huge red generator.

"It's not on yet," Vince said, rather proudly. "It's pretty loud. We figured we'd wait until we're finished setting up. Then we can plug in our cell phones, boot up the computers and even shed some light."

Tam saw he'd gotten a couple of standing lamps. Nothing matched, but it was all serviceable.

"Where do I put these?" she asked, raising the duffel bags.

"Over here." Nate led her to a hallway, then through another door; a completely different apartment. That kitchen also had a camp stove, a cooler, a coffee pot.

The living room had a table and chairs, two lamps and a loveseat. "Wow."

"This is our room," Nate said from yet another hallway. She passed a bathroom she'd never enter in this lifetime to a fairly decent room that had a small closet. It hadn't been swept yet, so she didn't put her things down. "I'll go find a broom."

"I'll take care of this," he said. "I need you and Kate to get together ASAP. We've got to get those ledgers transcribed."

She nodded, put the bags on the table in the living room and made her way to the computer room.

It was good to have so much to do. She'd never been much of a camper, and she missed a decent bathroom most of all, but by nightfall, they had food, beds, drinks, lights and she and Kate were knee-deep in work.

NATE WATCHED HIS TEAM come together and it made him proud. No one complained, not even Christie, which shocked him. He remembered her teenage years, when she'd been a regular little princess. Now she was in charge of dinner, and she was cooking up MREs like no one's business.

Still, something was wrong. Not just the fact that Cade wasn't here, but the fact that no one was talking about him. Something needed to be done. Tonight.

They ate at the big tables. Everyone pitched in, but it was too quiet. He tried several times to start conversations, but they all ran out of steam. Then he asked Kate about the ledgers. They'd be done tonight. Tomorrow, Vince would get a printer and they'd run copies. Nate just wished they had phone service out here. It complicated things, but what the hell. It would all work or it wouldn't.

When dinner was over, they mostly just threw stuff away and the place was as clean as it was likely to get. Before the team dispersed, he asked them each to get a flashlight and follow him.

As if they knew this was something important, they moved quickly and quietly. Nate led them into the desert, away from what remained of the old mining town.

It was almost a full moon, which helped them see as they walked past the scrub and the cactus. All manner of insects and lizards scurried out of their path, even a big old hare.

He didn't take them far, just away and when he stopped, they gathered round him in a circle. Tam was at his side, which made it all easier.

"It's only right and proper that we say a few words about our friend Cade. I first met him when he came over to Delta six years ago. For those of you who don't know, getting into Delta Force isn't an easy thing to do. You have to be smart, patient, strong and sure. Most of the men who come to visit us at Fort Bragg are in the prime of their lives. They come from every branch of the armed service, and they come decorated. But most of them wash out before they get their insignias. Being a Delta operator is an honor and a privilege known by few.

"Cade came from the Rangers. He was an excellent sharpshooter, but he wanted to be the best there was. He ran the forty miler in twenty hours. The day he became a member of the First Special Forces Operational Detachment, Delta, was the proudest day of his life.

"When I was asked to lead a team into Kosovo, I handpicked the men to go with me. Cade was right there in the front row. He had become the best damn sharpshooter I've ever known, and I've known quite a few.

"When things went south, Cade never lost his faith in his country. He believed in the United States of America, and just as he had when he came into Delta, he was willing to give his all to make sure that our America was a good America. That no group of people—no matter how powerful—can take it upon themselves to disregard the Constitution. That any group of people who should do so would be brought to justice.

"Cade Huston made the ultimate sacrifice for our country and our cause. He walked into battle each day knowing he faced danger and death, and he walked in with pride in his heart and the kind of courage the men we're fighting have never witnessed.

"We've lost our brother. I will never forget Cade, and I will make sure the American people understand that Sergeant Huston was and is a hero. He will not have died in vain. We will do what needs to be done."

# *13*

EVERY TIME JANICE'S PHONE rang, Eli was tempted to disconnect, but he kept his cell to his ear and waited. He was finally doing it, finally calling her. Janice Tucker was the love of his life, and if he lived to be one hundred, she'd still be the woman of his dreams. Unfortunately, he hadn't seen her since their high school graduation.

Still he could picture her in high definition detail. Her hair was the color of sun-dappled wheat and it hung thick and straight just past her shoulders. Her eyes were green with tiny specks of gold, which he'd noticed when they were chemistry lab partners. Her skin… It was perfect and although he'd never actually touched her, he just knew it would feel like silk.

It rang again, and he relaxed a little. She wasn't home so he could leave a message. He'd written it out, after about twenty false starts, and he'd practiced the words enough that he thought he sounded pretty natural.

All he had to do was not think about her body, because that flustered him every time. She was like a Playboy centerfold. Not that he'd ever seen her without her clothes, but she had a lush curvy body. And—

"Hello?"

It was her.

"Hello?"

"Janice?"

"Yes. Who is this?"

God, her voice was just the same. "It's Eli. Eli Lieberman."

"Who?"

"From high school? You know, chemistry? And English. You used to ask me for my notes?"

"Oh, yeah, sure. Eli. Hi. Are you on the reunion committee?"

"Reunion? No. I'm just calling."

"About…"

"Well, we both still live in Los Angeles, and I'm working for the *Times* now as a reporter, and—"

"You want to interview me about the reunion?"

"Well, no. I was wondering if you would like to get together for lunch, say at Jozu on Sunset, and then we could take a ride up the coast. I just got a new Turbo 911, and—"

"Um, Eli?"

"Yeah?"

"I'm actually seeing someone right now. And he's, you know, the jealous type. But hey, I'll make sure you get an invitation to the reunion, okay?"

"Yeah, sure," he said, and even he could hear his pathetic disappointment. "Nice talking to you."

"You, too. Bye now."

With that, she was gone, and so was his dream. The next time she heard about Eli Lieberman, it would be on the news reporting his death. She'd be sorry then, because he'd be famous. And she could have gone out with him.

His phone, still on, beeped with a new call. It was Nate. "What's going on?"

"You need to be at the meeting point tomorrow at 0600 hours."

"I'll be there."

"Good job, kid. I hope this gets you your Pulitzer."

"Thanks," he said, even though the Pulitzer would come way too late to make Janice feel worse, but he appreciated the thought. "Good luck. To all of you."

"Ten-four."

Eli disconnected and looked around his snazzy new apartment. It was small but it cost a fortune. Mostly for the address, but also for the décor. It was all ultra-modern by some guy who had a decorating show on HGTV. Eli liked it. Well, mostly. He was always slipping off the damn leather couch.

He had no reservations about the car. It was pure heaven. And yeah, most of his savings was gone, but that was okay. He'd made the arrangements to complete his part of the mission, even if he was killed.

NATE PUT HIS CELL PHONE away and looked at his team. They were still in what Boone had called the nerve center. No electricity except for the generator, no running water. It was a hell of a place to stage a final battle.

The memorial for Cade had done exactly what he'd hoped. He needed these people to walk into the very heart of hell. He doubted they would all live. In fact, it was highly unlikely that any of them would. They knew the odds, and they still had to carry out the complex mission without losing it. He didn't need to tell them their lives were secondary to the main goal of preventing Omicron from ever using the gas again.

What was so hard for him was that he needed all of them. Even the civilians. His sister. Harper. Kate. And Tam. He simply didn't have enough soldiers to get the job done. Especially now that they didn't have Cade.

He kept trying to think of a legitimate reason for leaving the women behind, but the four men couldn't possibly do everything necessary to win the day. Maybe he just wasn't seeing things clearly. He'd go over the plan again with Boone and Seth, see if they had any ideas. He was damn sure they didn't want Christie and Harper to face such incredible odds.

But tonight, Boone and Seth had to go back to the plant. It was inevitable that security would have changed the timing of the patrols since they'd caught Cade. And since it was highly likely that the guards had found the breach in the gate, the men would have to make a new entrance.

He debated going with them, but if something happened, he'd have to rethink the plan and figure out a way to save the women and Vince. It wasn't in his nature to sit back while others did the dirty work. He'd never wanted to be the one handing out the orders. He'd trained to be a soldier, the guy in the trenches. Watching his men leave was torture.

He'd go over the plans again, even though he knew

everything by heart. When the guys came back, he'd run it through again. After that, there was no turning back, and everything would have to run like clockwork.

He went over to the coffee pot and poured himself a cup, and saw that Seth and Boone had taken Harper and Christie to other rooms. Kate and Vince were on their way out, and Tam turned to him, looking unsure and a little frightened. He put his coffee down and went to her side. "Tired?"

She nodded. "You must be, too. You've had so little sleep."

"I'll get some rest after the guys head out."

She looked at her watch. "They'll be leaving in half an hour."

"I need to go over a few things, anyway. Do you want to wait, or would you be okay getting into that sleeping bag alone?"

"I think I'll wait, if that's okay."

"Sure. You want to check out the plan with me?"

She smiled. "I'd like that."

IT WAS TERRIBLE WATCHING Seth and Boone drive away. They were all thinking of Cade, and praying that come the dawn, they'd see these two men come back unharmed.

Tam looked up at the night sky, and was stunned at the blanket of stars. How long had it been since she'd been so far away from civilization that she could see the Milky Way? She was so tiny, so insignificant, and yet her feelings filled her whole universe. How was that possible? Was it ego? Or was it just the human condition?

"Beautiful, isn't it?"

Though Nate was standing next to her, she couldn't see him clearly. But she felt him. Felt the heat from his body, despite their coats. Felt the rasp of his unshaven cheek. He'd become such a huge part of her universe. By the day after tomorrow, everything would change once more. If she made it, she'd leave for home as quickly as possible. She wondered if he'd loom as large once they were out of this desert. Out of danger.

She wondered if she'd ever stop wanting him.

She found his hand and tugged him back into the big room. She turned off a few of the lights, then took him back to their so-called apartment.

"I really should go over—"

She put her fingers over his lips to stop him. "Make love to me."

His brow furrowed as he studied her face. "Are you sure that's what you want?"

She nodded. "Please. Just for tonight, let's pretend we don't have to save the world. Let's just be together."

"I'm so sorry," he said.

"For what?"

"I should have found a way to make you safe."

"That's exactly what you did."

"I don't want you to go into that plant. We can do it without you. We'll be fine."

She grasped his large hands. "We will be fine, but I'll be there. Doing my part."

"Tam—"

"Just for tonight. Please?"

He took her by the shoulders and pulled her close.

His arms went around her and she felt his chin rest on the top of her head. That always made her smile, their disparity in size, but tonight she realized it was yet another memory she'd take with her, and maybe some-day it would make her smile instead of weep.

He stepped back and lifted her chin for a kiss, and the second his lips touched hers, she knew she'd made the right decision.

She wasn't doing this for the good of the team. She was here because she cared deeply about this man. He'd been her world for so long. He'd given her so very much. Tonight, she'd do her best to take his mind off his burdens. She'd give him peace, even if it was only for a moment.

She pulled back and looked at the sleeping bags on the floor. "Kind of makes you miss the Starlight Motel."

He smiled. "It won't be so bad. Look." He unrolled one of the bags and she saw there was a foam cushion wrapped with it. Not that it would be like a bed, but it would help.

The second bag also had the foam. She pictured them sleeping on the cushions with the bags on top, but Nate did some tricks with the zippers so they had a double layer of insulation between them and the floor.

"Not bad, Sarge."

"I do my best."

She undressed carefully, placing her clothes on top of the duffel bag. She thought about the sad little night-gown she'd bought at Goodwill. With luck, she'd have nice things again. Lingerie. Boots. Jeans that really fit.

When they were naked and shivering, he maneuvered them both inside their bed. He cradled her neck on his arm, and then he kissed her. He tasted like peppermint, and he smelled like the desert itself. There simply was no better combination.

His free hand moved down the front of her body, lingering over each breast, then down to the edge of her mound. To her surprise, he moved up again, content with the languorous massage as they kissed.

She touched him, too. His shoulder, his arm, the curve of his chest and his hip. He'd left one light on, in the corner of the room, but in their bag it was very dark. When she closed her eyes she saw sparkling colors, so she kept them open, wanting no distractions. She just wished she could see him better. Good thing she'd memorized his face.

As his kisses grew deeper and more intense, she found herself urging his hand to go lower. Raising her hips, spreading her legs. She wanted him intensely, and she didn't give a damn why.

That thought opened a floodgate of all the reasons she was being a fool, and the only way she could stop them was to take his hand from her hip and guide it where she wanted him to go. He gasped a little as she used her own fingers to demonstrate.

Nate had always been a quick study, thank goodness. The second she felt the pad of his finger on her clit, she let him go solo. She turned just far enough to give herself access to his erection. She'd felt him rubbing against her, and it had felt so good, but it wasn't nearly enough. She took him in hand, loving the way he jumped as she gripped him.

This was it, the total immersion she'd been looking for. No more thinking. All thinking had ever done was get her into trouble. But feeling? Especially when the sensations were enough to drive her insane? That she could do. Hell, she could revel in those for days.

"You drive me crazy," he whispered. He took her earlobe between his teeth and his breath made her shiver.

"Then I'm doing it right," she said.

"I'm going to have to do something about your hand," he said.

She stroked him all the way up, then down again, and she didn't stop there. She rolled his sack in her hand, gently of course, but from his hiss, she knew he had no objections. If it hadn't been so difficult to move around, she'd have gone down on him, but this would have to suffice.

He got even with her, though. He pulled his hand back for a moment, then a second later he plunged two thick fingers inside her.

She yelped and maybe she got a little carried away because he yelped too, but not in a good way.

Immediately, she calmed down, but Nate just laughed, making her break out in goose bumps. "Watch the boys," he said. "I'm not finished with them yet."

"Sorry."

He continued to thrust into her. "That's okay. You'll make up for it."

"I will?"

"Yep."

"Just what were you thinking?"

"I want you to turn over."

"Oh, no."

His fingers stopped. "It's not what you think."

God, she wished she could see his eyes. "Promise?"

"I'd never do anything you didn't want."

"How do you know I'll want this?"

"Trust me," he said. "Now turn over."

She turned, but when she was on her side, facing away from him, he stopped her. "Here?"

"Perfect." He moved her top leg up, so it was bent at the knee. His lips moved to her neck, the sensitive skin just under her ear. As he nipped and licked, he guided his cock inside her. He moved slowly until he found his rhythm. Then, as she was savoring the sensation of him from behind, his fingers came back for an encore.

He used his finger, the most talented one, to find her clit, which he circled with the perfect amount of pressure. All the while, he moved in and out with his thick cock. That, combined with the things his tongue and teeth were doing, and she was approaching overload.

The only problem was her own hands. She really couldn't do much but hang on.

"Oh, my God," she said.

He chuckled, and she felt the vibration on her neck. Then, the devil took it to the next level. He started thrusting faster, moving his finger more quickly and the little nips on her neck were turning into bites that made her tense, followed immediately by long, slow laps of his tongue.

She had no idea if her eyes were open or closed, but

damned if she wasn't seeing fireworks. She felt her own body tense as he drew her closer and closer to orgasm. Her gasps turned to some weird, high pitched whine that she had no control over whatsoever. And her hands gripped the sleeping bag so tightly she was sure she had ripped it.

She held her breath as the moment came, that split second between anticipation and fulfillment. Her body rocked in a spasm as she came.

He moved his finger away from her sensitized clit, but pressed down on that area with his palm, holding her in position as he thrust again and again. It was an amazing sensation, the pressure, the fullness, the way her body trembled and she wanted so much to grab onto him that she brought her hand around and back, her fingers digging into his hip.

When he came, he cried out, a long, low growl incredibly loud so close to her ear.

They pressed against each other for a long time, until he collapsed with a whoosh and she gasped for breath.

Minutes went by as they both cooled off, which wasn't easy with him still inside her. Eventually, they settled. He was incredibly gentle and thoughtful in their cramped bed. He was the one to climb out, to wipe up, to make sure she was curled and cuddled right next to him when pure exhaustion made it difficult to keep her eyes open.

"Thank you," he whispered as he kissed her temple.

"I'll remember this always," she said. As much as she wanted to keep reality at bay, there were things to be said before all hell broke loose tomorrow. "You saved my life. You were my rock, my touchstone. If it wasn't for you, I wouldn't have known what it is to truly make love. You've given me so much."

He kissed her again. "Don't say it like it's over. We'll be fine, and we'll make love again. In a real live bed."

She knew her eyes were closed when she felt the tears on her lashes. "When it's over, I'm going home. And you're going on with your life."

"Tam—"

"It's true, Nate. You've been amazing, and I'll always be grateful, but we both have to find our lives again. You know I'm right. I just need you to know that I don't take it lightly. I've loved being with you. I don't blame you for my parents. Or for any part of this. No matter what, you're my hero."

He didn't say anything. But his body stiffened, and his hand left her back.

# 14

THE DAY STARTED at 4:00 a.m. Not just for Vince, who had the bulk of the errands to run, but for everyone. Boone and Seth were expected back by five-thirty and everyone had been anxiously awaiting their safe return since the moment they'd left.

In the central room, there was a pot of coffee and some oatmeal warming on the stove for breakfast. Nate was just back from a short sunrise run in the desert. It was the last he'd allow himself to think of Tam until the mission was complete. He'd left her in their room after a fitful night, one that had left him with more questions than answers.

He went into the apartment toting a gallon of water and some fresh clothes and he washed in an unoccupied room. Refreshed and hungry, he went back to join the others. Tam was at one of the tables with a cup of coffee, and the smile she gave him only increased his confusion.

But he'd think about her later. When they'd won. He was hungry, but he sat down with Christie and Harper, who both looked as if they hadn't slept at all.

"It's still early," he said.

Christie nodded. "It's a nice try, Nate, but we're not going to feel any better until they're back. Why don't you go talk to Vince. He's ready to head out, but I think he wants to go over the plan one more time."

He took his sister's advice, and found Vince by his truck with Kate. "You all set?"

"I think so. I know where I'm meeting Eli. I know what I'm picking up. I should be back before three."

"Call if there's any questions, and give Eli a pep talk, will you? He sounded pretty crappy when I spoke to him."

"The kid's done a good job so far."

"He needs to hear it again."

Vince shook his hand. "Will do, boss. You know this is going to work, right?"

"Ten-four."

"What is it you guys say? Lock and load?" Vince asked as he pulled Kate into his arms.

"Just get back here in one piece," Kate said.

Nate left them, feeling too much like Eisenhower on the eve of D-Day. But he knew that his talk yesterday had done some good.

He sat rereading his notes as he ate breakfast, willing himself not to check his watch. But he knew that it was coming on five, and that the men should be on their way. Damn it, he hated not having cell service. But he trusted them to—

Christie's "Truck!" had him on his feet, and they all watched as two men drove up the deserted road. They looked tired and filthy, but they were smiling to beat the band.

Nate breathed again and watched the homecoming with as much apprehension as joy. This was only the beginning.

VINCE SAT AT THE CORNER of Horizon Ridge and Highway 15. He was watching for an old Toyota Camry and barely noticed the guy in the red Porsche. Even when Eli stepped out of the car, it took Vince a minute to register who it was. "Hit the jackpot, did we?"

Eli blushed as he went around to open his trunk. "I've got everything you asked for."

"Great. Did you give Pat my message?" Pat was one of his less savory friends from his days in Vice.

Eli's blush returned. "He said to tell you to go fuck yourself."

"That's Pat. Let me see."

There was a large manila envelope sitting in the pristine trunk. Inside were seven ID badges. They weren't like the crap they'd rigged in the warehouse during Rodney Hammond's kidnapping. These were the real McCoy. They were for entry to Nellis, the real base, which they needed to get access to Omicron's little corner. Pat, one of the best forgers Vince had ever seen, had worked his usual magic. There would be no questions, not from any of the guards.

"These are terrific. Now, what about the rest?"

It took about ten minutes for the men to transfer the equipment to the bed of Vince's truck. He put a tarp over everything and tied it so tight no wind would dare creep inside. Then he handed Eli the most precious cargo of all. "They're labeled so you don't mix them up."

"Jesus, there's a lot of pages."

"There's a lot to tell."

"It took a hell of a lot of convincing to get the editor-in-chief to go along with all this. If you guys screw up, I'm toast at the *Times*."

He slapped Eli on the shoulder. "Don't worry about it, kid. You'll be dead before he can fire you."

Eli blanched, and Vince said, "Hey, seriously. We'll get through, and we'll get it done. You just be ready."

"I will."

"You've done great. Just keep on thinking of that Pulitzer."

The reporter didn't seem all that convinced he wasn't going to meet his maker in the next few hours.

"They'll be so busy trying to get us, they won't even be thinking of you. You're gonna be the next Woodward and Bernstein, all in one. Just hold on to that."

"I'll try. I'd better get back. There's still a lot to do before tomorrow."

Vince shook his hand. "You'll mostly be communicating with Christie, but I'll give you a holler when I can."

Eli nodded, then went back to his Porsche.

The sad ass thing was, Vince really didn't know if any of them would live through this. He just had to remember what he was fighting for.

THE WHOLE TEAM GATHERED just before midnight. Most of them had gotten at least some sleep, and they'd gone over every minute of the next ten hours as well as every single piece of equipment until each member of the team could pick up the slack if something went wrong.

Tam knew her own part in tonight's play, but she also knew that despite their planning and determination, the whole business could come to a deadly halt with one wrong step.

She was terrified that she'd be the one to screw things up. The rest of them looked so sure, so able. She couldn't stop her hands from trembling.

But she listened, she rehearsed until she was as ready as she'd ever be.

They were leaving in a few minutes, and if things went well, she doubted they'd be back. Her duffel was packed with only the essentials. Everything else would stay here until some lost soul happened upon the building. She wasn't sorry to let any of it go. She'd grown accustomed to leaving her life behind.

"Okay, team," Nate said. "Let's lock and load."

Those were the words they'd all been anticipating, but now that they were ready to go Tam was really glad she'd eaten such a light supper.

They were taking two trucks at least part of the way. She would ride with Nate, Harper, Kate, Christie and Vince. Boone and Seth were heading off first.

She checked to make sure the safety was engaged on her weapon, then she got in the passenger side of the truck. The four others climbed in the truck bed along with the equipment, and Nate got behind the wheel.

"You okay?" he asked, as soon as they were on the road.

"No. I'm scared to death."

"Not surprising. But you're gonna be great."

"Don't be so sure."

He looked at her, surprise in his eyes. "Are you kidding me? I've seen what you can do. Remember, I was there in Kosovo, when you had to run that gauntlet of gunfire to get in the jeep. I saw you in the cloud chamber, when all hell was breaking lose. And man, you made it out of the lab when two professional killers were after you. This isn't going to stop you."

She looked away, but only because she realized Nate meant what he was saying. It wasn't a pep talk, it was his truth. He thought she was strong. Capable. He was impressed not only by her brains but by her bravery.

"Tam?"

"No, I'm okay. Thank you."

He touched her leg. "Nothing's going to happen to you." He looked at her once more, this time with a ferocity she'd only seen a few times before. "I won't let anything happen to you."

Her hand covered his. And while she wouldn't allow herself to think past this night and tomorrow, she wished, for just a moment, that things were different between them. That they'd met under normal circumstances. And that she knew for sure the feelings she had for him were really love.

Seth pulled the truck into the rear of the Renegade parking lot. From the jam of cars it was obvious there was a big crowd in the bar. Country music could be heard along with the hum of chatter and laughter.

Boone nodded toward a four-door sedan, something dark and nondescript. Seth stopped the truck in front of the vehicle, blocking it from view. Boone jumped out, got behind the wheel and about twenty seconds later, the engine came to life.

It was just another specialty he'd learned in Delta. Although he'd never used it on an auto owned by a civilian, it was just like riding a bike.

Behind him, Seth backed up, and when Boone pulled out, they traded parking spots. Seth got in the sedan and Boone settled in for the ride. It would take them twenty minutes to get to the Vegas entrance of Nellis. Once inside, this nice little sedan would be left behind. But for now, he turned on the radio, and he thought about taking Christie home to meet his folks. As for Seth, he looked like he was planning his homecoming, too.

THEY RENDEZVOUSED AT A truck stop by the Vegas Speedway. Only Boone and Seth were no longer in the sedan. They'd each driven up in a regulation jeep, stolen from the Nellis motor pool.

It was 2:30 a.m., and all hands got out to transfer the equipment into the jeeps. This was the big one, and every one of them was as focused as a laser.

Once the jeeps were ready, they parked the truck. It took another thirty minutes for everyone to go in and use the johns because no two people walked in together. Nate hoped like hell this was the last night he'd have to sneak around like a fugitive.

And even that hadn't been as bad as pretending to be dead. After he'd come back from Kosovo, he'd started uncovering the truth about what had happened there. Once he'd realized just how bad things were, he'd staged his own death, complete with his sister as a witness. It had been agony to put her through that, but he was trying to keep her safe. Keep her clean. He'd hoped his apparent death would put an end to Omicron's search for those who'd escaped. For a while, it seemed as though his plan had worked. Then he'd discovered what those bastards had done to Christie.

Setting her up as a stalking victim had been bad enough, but the pricks had stolen all her money. They'd figured out a way to seize her bank accounts. That one had Senator Raines's fingerprints all over it.

So he'd come back to this half life. Living in squalor, hiding in shadows. He'd always been so proud of what he did, who he was. They'd taken that from him, too.

Once everyone was back in the jeeps, they headed northwest, toward the Omicron plant. Tam sat closer to him on this leg of the journey, but they still didn't talk much.

He wanted to. He wanted to say a lot of things, but she could distract him like nothing else.

He looked at her, sitting so still, staring straight ahead while her palm warmed his hand. Her quiet beauty got to him every damn time he saw her, and this morning was no different. It astonished him that she wasn't aware of her own strength. She'd been through hell and had kept her head on straight. Even now, she didn't know if her parents were living or dead. But she had practiced her part over and over until she knew it by heart.

He had stopped trying to pretend he wasn't in love with her. She was everything he wanted in a partner. Kind, smart, funny, sexy as hell. He wanted to have kids with her. He'd never had that thought before, not with anyone.

But she was right. While he'd had more life than any two people he knew, she really had no idea who she was, or what she was capable of. She deserved to find out without him getting in the way.

"You're thinking about us," she said.

He sat back, knowing he hadn't said any of that aloud. "What?"

"I can see it on your face. You're thinking about us, and your hand is rubbing my leg, and while I think that's incredibly sweet, you need to knock it off."

He looked down to find his hand had traveled all the way to the top of her thigh. "Shit. Sorry."

"It's okay. You can pick up the thread when this is over, and tell me all about it."

"Can I?"

She smiled. "I didn't say I didn't want to speak to you again."

"I know, but—"

"Nate. Concentrate." She lifted his hand and put it in his own lap. Then she scooted to the far edge of her seat.

"Yes, ma'am."

He kept driving, keeping to the speed limit, and all he thought about was finally stopping Omicron once and for all.

ABOUT A MILE from the plant, both jeeps turned off the highway and drove across some rough desert. Seth went over the plan again and again, and tried to prepare himself for any eventuality.

He didn't want to die tonight. He'd found Harper, and the two of them had so much more to say to each other. So much more to do. He wanted to see her as a doctor again. She loved her work and she was damn good at it. He'd never go back to the soldier's life. That was over. He didn't blame the good men and women in the service, but these past couple of years had taken the fight right out of him. And with his claw, he doubted they'd want him back.

But he and Nate and Vince had been talking. Between them, they had one hell of a lot of skill. When this was over, they'd use them, starting their own security firm. Where they'd get the money, he had no idea, but it would happen. Because they'd be free men. And women. Christie and Kate were included in the package, and he was fine with that. They were both sharp and smart, and they knew a little something about covert ops.

The future looked bright. He just had to live, that's all. Live and fight for one more day.

He knew they were getting close to the fence they'd prepped last night. He checked his weapon as Boone pulled the jeep to a stop. "You ready?" Boone asked.

"Let's do it."

They got out of the jeep, leaving the key in the lock. With one last look at the team, at the women they loved, they checked the time, and knowing the guards wouldn't be patrolling by for seven more minutes, they crawled through the gap in the fence and started off across the desert, double-time.

NATE CHECKED HIS WATCH AS the men disappeared into the night. The rest of the team had climbed out of the truck bed, and Vince took over the driver's seat. But they wouldn't be going anywhere, not for a while. Not until they got the signal.

He got out of the jeep and walked, stretching his legs, his neck and back. He hated this part. The waiting was torture, always had been. But one thing you learn in the service is patience.

About ten minutes in, he took out his walkie-talkie. It was a small unit, not regulation in any way, but for this operation it was perfect. Although it looked like a toy, the range was exceptional. Each member of the team had one, but there was only one voice he wanted to hear.

"They should be there by now," Christie whispered. She had her arms folded across her chest and she was shivering. It was cold out, but not freezing. He figured it was fear for Seth that made her tremble.

"They have to be very careful."

"I know, but still. Shit. I hate this, Nate. I hate this plan with all my heart."

He drew her to him in a bear hug. "These are the best soldiers I know. If anyone can get through it, they can."

"But you don't know. After Cade, they could have changed everything about their security."

"Trust me, Boone's seen a lot worse. He's gotten out of scrapes you wouldn't believe."

"I don't want to know."

They stood for a few minutes, rocking gently back and forth. He was crazy about his little sister, and all he wanted for her was the best. He wasn't crazy about bringing her along on this trip, but as with Tam, there was no choice.

"You gonna go see Mom and Dad?" she asked.

"I suppose so."

"She'll want you to."

"I know. I just—"

"We don't even know if Dad's still alive. He wasn't looking so well the last time I saw him."

"I'll go. But I may have to take care of some business first."

"With Tam?"

"No. With the U.S. Government."

She stepped back and looked up. "Is Tam going with you?"

"No. Tam is going home. She's lost a lot of her life. It'll take time for her to find it again."

"Wait a minute. Are you kidding? You're good with her, Nate. I've never seen you like this. You can't walk away from her."

"I—" He stopped at a crackle from the walkie-talkie. He held it up and listened, the rest of the team gathering around.

He wanted—more than anything—to say something. To ask Boone what was going on. But he figured it out when he heard Boone scream.

## 15

HE HAD TO GRAB CHRISTIE before she crumpled to the ground. Her sobs hit him in the gut, and he cursed himself for being every kind of a fool. He'd just stood here and let them listen. Harper wasn't crying, but she was so still he thought she might pass out.

Pulling Christie into his arms, he felt her body spasm against him. He'd made a mistake, and this one might end the mission right here. "Honey? Christie? Come on, look at me."

She shook her head and she hit him in the chest. "You let them do this!"

"Christie, you need to listen to me. Just for a minute. We don't know anything. We don't know why Boone screamed like that."

"Because he was being murdered!"

"No, that's only one scenario, and the most unlikely one at that. Boone's been in this kind of situation before, and he's going to use every trick in the book to get what he wants. That scream could have been to get someone's attention, to fake them out so he could strike. He could have been warning Seth, or scaring someone into losing their aim. I've seen it done before, so please, do not give up on him. He needs you now. He needs all of us."

"You're lying. You're lying so you don't have to face me."

"I swear to you, I'm not. You're his partner. You have to hang tough."

She wiped her face with her sleeves. "I'm an interior decorator. You hear me? I'm not a soldier. I never wanted to be. You ask too much."

"I ask what I have to. We can't live the rest of our lives as fugitives. We can't let them kill more people."

"That wasn't the scream of someone playing a trick."

"If Boone was really in trouble, we would have heard something else."

"What?"

"The grenade."

That stopped her. She hiccupped and wiped her face again, but the wracking sobs had stopped. "If you're lying to me, I swear to God, Nate Pratchett, I'll kill you myself."

"Save that anger for the bad guys. Now come on. We have work to do."

TAM WATCHED AS NATE AND Vince started cutting the fence. They used wire cutters and the lights from the jeep to guide them, because if they made a mistake, they'd fry. Literally. It all had to be done incredibly fast, too, because of the frequent patrols.

But all she could think about was how the world had turned upside down yet again.

A moment before that horrible scream, she'd been

awash in her own fear, coaching herself to keep breathing, trying hard to remember everything she'd learned in the last couple of days. To remember her part. By the time Christie had collapsed in Nate's arms, she wasn't afraid at all. Not for herself, at least. She realized the thing that would truly hurt her, kill her, would be losing Nate.

It took all her energy and courage to keep from running away as fast as she could. It would be better not to know, that's what she told herself, but it wasn't true. She had no idea what would happen after tonight. The only thing that mattered was that they all made it out alive. In order to do that, she had to perform to the best of her ability. No weeping, no closing her eyes. She was Nate's partner. She was a member of this team. She could do this.

The minute the fence had been cut wide and high enough for the jeeps to get through, Nate turned out the lights and had everyone but Vince climb in their assigned vehicles. Then the two men slipped through the wire. Like Boone and Seth, they disappeared into the darkness seconds after they were on the other side.

Tam was in the passenger seat, with Harper in the rear. Tam turned to the doctor. "Are you okay?"

"I won't be okay until I see Seth."

"I understand."

Harper looked away toward the empty desert. "I didn't mean to fall in love with him, you know. He was a royal pain for a real long time."

"What happened?"

"He saw through me. He saw that I was all bluster

and walls, and he just kept on pushing. Eventually, I gave up."

"That's good."

"I'm not so sure. Not tonight. I was never this scared before Seth. No one's ever been this close to me, and there's a lot that's not so great about that."

"But the good parts, they make it worth it, right?"

"They did. If something does happen to Seth, you can bet your life I'll never go through this again. It's too much."

"Seth has a lot to live for. He's not going to give in easily."

Harper nodded, and looked away for a moment, clearly trying to get a grip on her emotions.

Tam turned to the gate, and she saw Nate and Vince come back through. They each held clothes in their hands, and in minutes they'd stripped off their civvies and donned two security uniforms. Nate's didn't fit so well, not over his chest, but it would do if no one looked too closely. They clipped on their ID badges, then got to work.

Nate took out the receiver and transmitter and set them in the front passenger seat of the lead jeep. Christie got behind the wheel where she'd stay for the remainder of the mission. He hated to leave her alone, but they needed someone to monitor the transmission that would be relayed from the plant to a server in Las Vegas and finally to the *Los Angeles Times*, where Eli had a DVR system all set up, ready to go.

She went over her instructions, and then she put her weapon and her walkie-talkie on her lap. Nate kissed her on the cheek. "I'll let you know the minute I find Boone."

"I'm counting on it."

He nodded, then he climbed in the second jeep. All the other equipment was there, and so was the rest of the team. It was a tight fit, but they weren't travelling far.

"You ready?" Nate asked. He didn't wait for an answer. They all ducked as the jeep went through the fence.

This was it. No turning back.


"MAKE SURE THEY DON'T move a muscle." Tom Cannon looked at the two men who'd been brought to him by his guards. He'd expected some action from these jokers, but not so soon after the other one had blown himself up. Despite the blood and swelling on their faces, Tom knew exactly who he had in his office. He could smell his promotion already.

He picked up the phone and dialed Leland Ingram's private line. He'd wake the old man up, but Ingram wouldn't mind. Not for this.

The phone rang as Cannon thought about finally getting out of this dump. He'd never wanted to work at the plant. He'd been a great agent in his day, and he wanted to be in the field. But Ingram had made him head of security, graveyard shift. The money was good, but he hated the desert. He hated working graveyard. His house was crap, the women in town were dogs and he didn't particularly like spending his nights on top of a powder keg.

The engineers had sworn up and down that the safest place he could be was in his office. That the walls and ceiling were made of aluminum, the same thing they used to contain the gas, and that if there was even the smallest leak, the upper floors would close up tight.

"Who is this?"

"It's Tom Cannon, Mr. Ingram." Jeez, he sounded pissed. "I've got two packages here."

There was a considerable pause. "Don't do anything. I'll be there within two hours."

"Yes, sir." Cannon hung up the phone and looked at his captives. They weren't going anywhere. He looked forward to seeing what Ingram had planned for them. It was going to be an interesting show.

INGRAM DRESSED AS QUICKLY as possible, then woke up the Omicron pilot who assured him the chopper was ready to go. It was a ten minute drive to Omicron's downtown L.A. headquarters, and he used that time to get his men rounded up. They'd take a second helicopter and meet him at the plant.

By the time he reached the helipad, the sun was just inching up on the horizon.

He buckled in. It wouldn't take long to get to Nevada. Once he was there, it also wouldn't take him long to make those bastards break. It was still too early to call Raines, but he was looking forward to that conversation. Shit, this was going to be a good day.

NATE STOPPED THE JEEP a quarter of a mile from the plant. They'd go the rest of the way on foot. They had four minutes until the next patrol, which wouldn't leave them enough time to unload, then camouflage the vehicles. He and Vince had the women crouch down as they unrolled some of the niftiest NISH desert camo tarp he'd ever seen. By the time the guards rolled by they'd see a sand dune that looked like all the other sand dunes, complete with sagebrush and cactus. The only thing missing were jumping lizards.

When he climbed under the tarp, the dark caught him by surprise. He'd barely noticed the scarlet sunrise. He would have preferred waiting it out on the ground, weapon ready, but he wasn't about to leave the women alone.

They were quiet for long, stressful minutes, and then they heard the sound of an oncoming jeep. He held his breath as the sound grew louder, then began to fade. He didn't let anyone move until they could hear nothing at all.

Then it was hustle time as everyone grabbed the gear. There was a lot, but none of it was too heavy. He made sure his hands were free to hold his Colt M4A1 rifle. Vince was more comfortable with his own Glock 9, but he'd been given a M4 as well. It was the weapon of choice for the Special Forces, and the rifles Omicron security carried.

They covered up the jeep again and headed toward the lab. He knew there were workers inside, but they wouldn't be a problem for long. It was Saturday, and the graveyard shift was just about to clock out. The worst of it would be getting inside the main door. But they'd all gone over this part of the plan a hundred times.

As they closed in on the plant, the backpacks were transferred to the women. Then he pulled Tam's arms behind her and encased her wrists in handcuffs.

She winced, and he wanted to kiss her like nobody's business, but he couldn't. Vince had cuffed Harper and Kate. They walked their prisoners toward the front entrance just as the employees started a steady stream out.

No one seemed too surprised that security had found trespassers. Nate felt sure by now they'd all heard about Cade, and likely the capture of Boone and Seth, too. Maybe they hadn't expected women, but no one stopped them. Of course, these were just the plant grunts.

They walked straight through the center of the lines to the chamber door. Vince took a keycard Boone had stolen, and the first door opened. There were still people hanging about, coming out of the locker rooms, talking and laughing.

Just as he was preparing to break into the inner sanctum, a voice behind him sent a chill down his spine.

"Who the hell are you?"

Nate turned, pushing back his shoulders and puffing up his chest. "Who's asking."

It was security, all right, dressed just like Vince and himself. He had his weapon up and aimed. "If I don't see badges in about two seconds, the coroner will be asking."

Nate snapped his ID off his shirt. "We're here on Mr. Ingram's orders, and he's gonna be here in about two minutes. If we're not up there, I'm gonna mention your name." He leaned to his left to see the man's badge. "George."

George studied the badge, then Nate's face. His lips pressed together, letting Nate know he wasn't totally convinced. "Who are they?"

"You want to know that," Nate said, snatching back his badge. "You talk to Mr. Ingram."

George's eyes narrowed. "Don't think I won't check up on this."

"You do that," Nate said, turning his back on the guard.

He heard footsteps retreating a moment later, then the look of relief on Harper's face. "Let's do this," he whispered.

The three women made a semicircle barrier to hide him as he got Rodney Hammond's glove out of Tam's pack. He slipped it on and pressed the hand on the scanner.

A few seconds later, the big door opened.

Even though he knew about the bombs, the sheer number of them made him lose a step. It was mass murder on an unimaginable scale. It was not a pleasant place to be, especially for the women who were cuffed. But they marched through, following the bright yellow line, until they reached the door to the clean room.

The only good thing about being here was the absence of witnesses. The place was freezing, thick vapor coming from all of the vents. Because it was the final staging area, unless they were loading or unloading, everyone who could stayed clear. But this room wasn't the problem.

He looked into the clean room. Inside were the consoles and computers that ran the plant. They could lock down the building with a push of a button, and if that happened, his team was dead.

A man in a white chem suit, minus the helmet, looked them over as they approached the door. He pressed a button on the console and his voice came out of a speaker. "What the hell's this?"

"We're supposed to bring them to Ingram."

"He's not here."

"He said to meet him inside."

The man frowned, but he pressed the right button, opening the door.

The women went in first. There were three men working there in addition to the guy who'd let them in. The second the door closed behind Vince, the women—as planned—hit the ground. Nate didn't think—he just shot the four men each with a clean shot. The last one had been close as the guy had lunged for the alarm.

Vince looked at him. "Holy shit. I didn't even get the goddamn safety off."

"I always said you homicide cops were pussies."

"We'll talk about that when this is over."

"Hey," Harper said. "You two can play later."

Nate and Vince got out the keys and removed the cuffs. Then they went to the back of the room where the heavy duty chemical suits were hung.

Harper got one down, and then Kate and Tam did the same, but they didn't put them on. Not yet. They took them to the main section of the clean room, and Nate walked over to the front console. There, he found what he was looking for—the controls for all the entrances and exits. He nodded at Vince, who went back into the bomb storage area. Three minutes later, Vince was back. "It's all clear. Now."

Nate pressed the button that turned off the biometric scanner. He locked the outside door, and even the ventilation shaft. The only thing he didn't lock was the elevator. No one was getting in or out without his say so.

He checked with Tam. "You okay?"

"I've got it," she said, as she held up the small camera. It was a beauty, the size of a paperback book, but it could broadcast a pristine picture with its miniature wireless transmitter. "Give me a test."

She held the camera steady as she aimed it out the window into the bomb room. Nate got on the walkie-talkie. "Christie? You getting this?"

"I am."

"Get on the horn with Eli. Make sure he's seeing it, too."

While he waited for Christie to come back, he helped Harper set up the microphone. Vince went to the bomb room again and did a sound check. All the meters looked operational, and then Christie came back with the all clear. The mission was a go.

Nate waved Vince in, and the two of them raced to the elevator. It was hell going up, counting the seconds, wondering if they'd find Boone and Seth alive, but they were ready when the door opened. With two single shots from two separate rifles the guards were down, and Nate and Vince were racing down the hall, throwing open doors that led to plush offices. Finally, they hit pay dirt and went in like a tornado.

There were five men aside from Ingram in the room. One goon was standing over Seth, fist raised for a blow that would knock down an elephant. He was the first man Nate shot.

Vince didn't lag behind this time. He took out two

of the guards. Nate had to smash one in the face with the butt of his rifle as he came from behind, then shoot the one pointing his automatic between his eyes. When he turned around, Ingram also had a gun in his hand, pointing it at Nate's chest. Vince clocked him in the back of the head.

He went down with a satisfying thud. Nate and Vince untied their men. They looked like shit, with bruises and cuts all over their faces. Seth's right eye was swollen shut.

"Jesus," Nate said. "Tell Harper to look for a first aid kit. A big one."

"Hell, I had worse at boot camp," Seth said, wiping the blood from his split lip.

"Let's get him out of here," Boone said, bending to lift Ingram.

"Hold on, soldier." He handed Boone his walkie-talkie. "Tell my sister you're okay and that you love her."

He broke out in a grin and clicked the button. "Christie? Honey?"

All they heard from the other end was crying. It was a really good sound.

"I'll see you in a little while," he said. "You just watch those monitors. And don't be afraid if you hear the sirens."

He signed off then gave the walkie-talkie back to Nate, who pressed the button again, this time asking for Tam.

"I'm here."

"We've got them. Hit the alarm."

A second later Klaxons went off from every speaker

in the plant, and Nate could just picture the panic it was creating. Whoever was left in the area wouldn't be there for long. Including the helicopter on the roof.

He and Vince got Ingram to his feet. They cuffed his hands behind his back and half walked, half dragged the dazed man to the elevator.

By the time he'd recovered his senses, he was tied to a chair in a room filled with bombs. Harper, wearing her chemical suit stood in front of him. She'd put the canister of gas at his feet.

Inside the control room, the camera rolled and the microphone picked up every syllable of Leland Ingram begging for mercy.

IN THE NEWSROOM AT THE *Los Angeles Times*, Eli Lieberman was trying his best not to have a heart attack. He had two of the fastest fax machines known to man running constantly to his right, a computer and DVR system complete with tech guys on his left and the freaking editor-in-chief was standing over his shoulder trying to tell everyone what they were doing wrong.

Half the faxes were going out to every news outlet in the country. They were receiving his and Corky Baker's background story, plus the complete breakdown of the money trail that led from Kosovo to Omicron to a bank account in the Cayman Islands and ended at the feet of Senator Jackson Raines.

The other fax machine was spitting out technical data to the Centers for Disease Control, the National Health Institute and every other chemical and pharmaceutical research facility in seven countries. They were getting the chemical composition of the antidote, as well as the background on the gas. The call was out to the finest scientific minds in the world to find a dispersal system for the antidote, to make sure no one on the planet ever died again from Omicron's gas.

And that was only the beginning.

# 16

Leland Ingram kept staring at the canister, his lips trembling and his eyes wild. He—above all others—knew what would happen to him if the canister should leak. But just in case he forgot something, Harper was there to remind him.

"Hey there, Leland. You don't know me personally, but you tried to have me killed, so I feel I can call you Leland. I'm that pesky doctor who witnessed that mass murder you bastards committed. But since you were so far away from the experience, we thought you might like to get a much better feel for what went down in Serbia. And in Chad."

She leaned closer to him. "Don't worry, Leland. You won't have to wait long to feel the effects. First, your pupils will constrict, so you might experience some visual difficulty. Then you'll get a headache and you'll feel a terrible pressure in your sinus cavities. Your nose will run and you'll probably drool. And that's all within the first minute."

She wished she could take off the chemical helmet because it made her voice sound funny and it wasn't easy to breathe, but that would ruin the effect. "Next," she said, "comes the tightness in the chest. You might think you're having a heart attack, which I suppose you are, at least to some degree. You'll vomit. A lot. Which won't seem half as bad as what comes next. I'm afraid it gets even messier. You'll urinate. And you'll defecate. Probably at the same time, and all within the second minute."

He was weeping now, and he wasn't even waiting for the gas to have a runny nose. "Please. Don't. I beg you." His voice wobbled and broke. It was so pathetic she wanted to laugh in his face.

She crouched down by the canister instead. "The one thing I'm pretty sure of is that the last part, the part before you die? That hurts like a son of a bitch. When I was in Serbia, in that village you wiped out, I looked at the children's faces. They died in excruciating pain, you evil prick. Even the people inside the houses, who didn't have the direct exposure to their skin, died horrifying deaths."

"It wasn't me. I swear to God, I was just following orders. I didn't know."

She put her hand on top of the canister, painted to look exactly like all the others in the bomb room.

"Wait."

It wasn't Ingram, it was Nate, right on cue. He was also in chem gear, and he no longer had his rifle.

"Why?" she asked.

"Give him a chance."

She stood. "Why should I? He didn't give any of those children a chance."

"I want to hear what he has to say." Nate turned to Ingram, still quivering and staring at the casing. "If it wasn't you in charge, who was?"

"Raines. Senator Raines. He's the man behind it all. I was just working for him."

Nate smiled behind his mask. One down, one to go. "Why did Raines have you use a Delta Force unit to wipe out all the scientists?"

"You were the best," he said. "And loyal. He didn't think you'd question your orders."

"But, Leland, weren't you going to kill us anyway?"

"He was!" Leland was almost insane with fear now.

"Tell me the plan, Leland." Nate kept his voice steady and calm. He didn't want Ingram passing out.

"Raines needed money. Millions. He needed to seed the campaigns of the congressional races where those sharing his vision were running for election. He wants control, and he wants to be president. But he couldn't get the amounts of money he needed by donations alone." Leland looked up briefly, but he couldn't stand it. He had to stare at the canister. "He figured he'd kill two birds with one stone. He never believed the U.S. should have signed the chemical weapons disarmament treaty. So he sent the scientists to Kosovo."

"And now he's used the gas twice, right? Once in Serbia and once in Chad?"

"Just take that thing out of here, and I'll tell you everything."

"That you will, Leland."

"SENATOR RAINES."

He looked up from his desk at the intrusion. It was Mark, his aide, and Mark wasn't the type to come barging into his office. The kid looked panicked, and Raines put his pen down. "What's happened?"

"Sir, you'd better turn on the news."

Raines picked up his remote and turned on one of the three televisions he had installed in the wall across from him. The first thing he saw was a picture of Leland Ingram. Raines felt his blood run cold as he made out where Ingram was. And that he was tied up next to a canister of the gas.

Below the picture, there was type scrolling, and he immediately saw his own name inch by.

With shaking fingers, he turned on the other two televisions, and the picture was all the same. Live. From Nevada. From the manufacturing plant that wasn't supposed to be on U.S. military property. Each one showed with shocking clarity the rows of bombs that weren't supposed to exist, containing a deadly chemical weapon that was banned by international treaty.

"Get the helicopter ready," he said.

"Yes, sir. But, sir?"

"What?"

"There are reporters outside. Lots."

Senator Raines leaned back in his chair. Even if he did leave, they'd find him. He'd be branded as a traitor, and his people, his loyal cohorts that had followed him from his humble beginnings as the mayor of Los Angeles, they would all scurry and hide. They'd name names and they'd turn on him so quickly they would leave skid marks. It was human nature.

He had no regrets about what he'd done. Only that he hadn't killed those damned Delta Force soldiers.

"Forget the 'copter, Mark," he said. "I'll be out to see the press in a moment."

"Yes, sir."

When Mark had closed the door, the senator opened his top drawer and reached in the back. The first pistol he'd ever bought felt good in his hand. It should. He polished it regularly and took it to the firing range more often than any of his other weapons.

He turned back to the TV set and watched Leland Ingram try to talk his way out of his imminent death. For a moment, Raines thought about waiting, watching Leland die. But in the end, he just wanted it over with.

TAM COULDN'T BELIEVE IT. She wanted a television so she could be sure, absolutely sure that what she was recording was really going on the air, and that there wasn't some horrible mix-up.

Boone's walkie-talkie crackled. It was Christie. Tam couldn't hear what she said, but Boone was grinning like a fool when he signed off. "The good guys are on their way. Eli called Christie. There's a boatload of law enforcement coming in from Vegas, along with a Hazardous Materials team. They're closing this place down, and taking that asshole in." He nodded toward Ingram who had no hesitation whatsoever in selling out every person he'd ever met.

Tam wished she could drop the camera right this second and get on the phone with her parents. Assuming…

No, she wouldn't go there. This was a wonderful day,

the best she'd had in years. The nightmare that had become her life was over. She could go home.

The only cloud was that meant leaving Nate. She didn't want to do that. She cared about him deeply. In fact, she was pretty sure she loved him.

But it was the *pretty sure* that told her she had to go.

Even in that horrible chemical suit, Nate looked like a leader. The way he stood over Ingram. His commanding voice, even through the distortion of the helmet.

She wondered what it would be like to wake up knowing Nate wasn't in the next room, or on an errand. She couldn't imagine it.

It was too hard thinking of the bad part, so she thought about the good. By this time, scientists and chemists all over the world would be reading her papers. They'd understand exactly what it had taken to create the antidote. Of course, they'd also know that she'd failed with the disbursement system, but those close to her field would realize how limited her resources had been.

She was still concerned about the reaction to her decision to go to Kosovo in the first place. Why hadn't she insisted they tell her what the work was for? Why hadn't she made it a point to talk to the other chemists?

She'd live with her guilt and regrets for the rest of her life. She promised herself that whatever work she did in the future, she would do her damnedest to make up for it, and make damn sure her work was for good ends, and the good of humanity.

"WE KNOW YOU HAVE AN ACCOUNT in the Cayman Islands, Leland. Do you think it's right that Senator

Raines should get away with all that money? Don't you think the families of those you killed deserve reparation?"

"Yes, yes. Please, God, I have to go to the bathroom. Let me go and I'll tell you the account number."

"Not gonna happen. Tell us the account number now, and then we'll untie you."

Ingram was sweating so profusely he looked as if he'd just stepped out of the shower, his pale hair plastered to his forehead, his shirt dripping. Nate wanted him to suffer more, much more. He wanted him to die by his own gas, but there was still enough of a soldier left in him that he couldn't do it, even though he knew he could make it look like a mistake.

"I can't. I can't tell you."

"You have the antidote?" he asked Harper.

She nodded and went to the door of the safe room where Boone handed the syringe to her. It was very large—a horse syringe, actually. Bought on one of Vince's scouting missions. And it was filled with nothing more than discolored water.

She came back in front of Leland and gave him a real good view. "I have to administer this within the first minute of exposure," she said. "In order for it to be effective, I'm going to have to inject you directly in the heart."

She put the syringe down and took off her thick gloves. She reached over the canister and ripped Leland's shirt open, the buttons clinking on the floor.

He gasped as if he'd been stuck through with a blade. As they watched, the crotch of his very expensive pants darkened.

Nate knew this would humiliate him, pissing himself on national television. It was a small thing, and petty, but he enjoyed the hell out of it.

"Well, I guess you won't have to worry about urinating when the gas hits," Harper said. "Or going to the bathroom."

He was sobbing now. No words, just body shaking, wrenching sobs. His pale skin quivered and his nose ran.

"Tell me the bank. The account number. And the balance," Nate said.

He wailed, but he didn't talk.

Nate nodded at Harper. She put her gloves back on and checked for exposure. Then she looked up at Nate. "You'd better clear out. I only have the one dose of antidote."

He nodded, hoping this would be the last of it. He went for the door as Harper put her hand down on the top of the canister.

"Wait! Jesus God, don't do it. I'll tell you, I swear."

Nate stopped. "Right now, Leland."

He gave them the information they wanted, but hesitated again when it got to the bank balance.

Nate started to leave again, and that was all it took.

"Two point eight billion."

"Did you say billion?"

"Yes. Billion."

"Holy crap." Nate shook his head, then headed inside the clean room, Ingram's screams begging him to stop.

He took off his helmet and looked at his team. No one was celebrating just yet. Boone and Seth were at the ready, despite the fact that Seth could hardly see. Tam stood by the window, aiming the camera with steady hands, and Kate was monitoring the meters, making sure nothing got cut off, or went screwy.

Vince, on the other hand, was sitting with his feet up on the console wearing a large smile as he watched the show. The only thing missing was his tub of popcorn.

"The cavalry is coming," Boone said. "Hazmat, the FBI. It's gonna be a regular dog and pony show."

"Look," Nate said, "we know they're going to want to take us back to Washington, but it's gonna take awhile for them to get their act together. What say we get the hell out of here while we can? We've got everything we needed on tape. Eli's handling the press. We'll let them know where we are when we're ready."

"Where do you want to go?" Harper asked.

"I don't know." Nate grinned. "But I'm thinking a cold beer might be real nice."

"I know where we can find exactly that," Boone said. "But maybe we should get Seth patched up before we celebrate. Oh, and we need to spring Milo, too."

"Seth?" Nate asked. "You need a hospital?"

"Hell no. I need a drink."

"Then it's a done deal."

He turned around and Harper was waiting for the signal. She nodded, then held up the syringe once more. "Leland, this is from all of us. Nate Pratchett, Christie Pratchett, Seth Turner, formerly known as Jeff Harris. Kate Rydell, also known as Kathryn Ashman. Vince Yarrow. Dr. Tamara Chen. The late Cade Huston, who his parents know as Charles Dugan, and me, Harper Douglas, who was licensed as Dr. Karen Clements. We're all looking forward to watching you go straight to hell."

She unscrewed the top of the container, and immediately vapor started rising from the can.

Leland screamed quite loudly. Of course he had no idea it was dry ice in the canister, not his precious gas. She wouldn't be at all surprised if he did have a heart attack, but that wasn't her problem. She hated this bastard and his suffering would never begin to make up for what he'd done.

She stood up with the syringe in her hand. He looked at her desperately, straining with all his might to break the ropes, and she was sure he was feeling at least some of the symptoms. She stepped closer. Smiled. And let the syringe drop.

It shattered at Leland's feet, but he didn't see it. He'd already passed out.

She took off her helmet, tired of being hot and sweaty. Nate had had to convince her that the dry ice would work. It really didn't look anything like the actual gas. He'd never have been able to see that or smell it.

Nate said he'd be so scared they could have shaken a can of Coke and sprayed it on him, and he would have believed he was about to die.

She spit, although it didn't reach him. Then she turned and joined her friends in the clean room. The moment she heard they were going to try to beat the troops, she was all for it. This was a private victory, one they more than deserved.

"WHAT ARE YOU STOPPING FOR?"

Nate pulled the truck over to the side of the road. They weren't even close to a town and they'd been watching a steady stream of vehicles, most with red lights and sirens, flash past them on their way to the plant.

"Look up there," he said, pointing to a mountain in the distance.

Tam didn't understand. "What am I looking for?"

"There's a cell tower. In our line of sight."

"Okay?"

"Honey, you can call your folks now."

Tears sprang to her eyes. "Really?"

He nodded, handing her his cell. "I charged it on the generator. It should last as long as you need it to." He opened his door.

"You're leaving?"

"I want to tell the others. They all have people to call. I'm sure our pictures are all over the news."

"What about you?"

"I'll talk to my mother after Christie's done. But you go ahead. If you need me, I'll be right out there."

He closed the door behind her. She had to call information to get the number at the San Francisco hospital, and then when she did, they didn't want to connect her to her parents' room. At least she knew they weren't dead, or she'd have been switched to the morgue. Finally, she convinced them to put the call through.

"Hello?"

It wasn't her mother's voice. "Is this Mrs. Chen's room?"

"Yes, it is. May I tell her who's calling?"

Tam hesitated. She didn't want to scare her mother if she hadn't been watching the news. "Are you a friend?"

"I'm her nurse."

"Good, then you can tell me. Has she been watching the news?"

"No, her television is off."

"Oh, dear."

"Who is this?"

"I'm her daughter."

"But—"

"I know. She thought something had happened to me. That I'd been killed."

"I see," said the nurse, hesitantly.

"Have you been watching the news?"

"Yes."

"You know that chemical plant? The one that was a secret government plot?"

"It's on every station."

"I was working on that. Undercover. So I couldn't tell them—"

"Okay, I'm getting it now. Hold on. She's just getting back from her shower."

"Wait. Please, is she going to be all right?"

"Yes, she is. And so is your father, although his injuries were a little more severe."

Tam had stopped trying to wipe the tears away. "Okay, I'm ready when she is. Just, would you stay with her, make sure she's okay?"

"Sure thing. One minute."

Tam shook as she waited, excited and desperate to hear her mother's voice.

"Oh, my God. Tam? Is it really you?"

She couldn't say anything. Not for a full minute. But finally, she said, "Yes, Momma. It's really me."

# 17

ELI STOOD IN THE MIDDLE of the newsroom as unbridled chaos swirled around him. It was just after two-thirty in the afternoon and he'd been up for twenty-six hours. He couldn't remember a time when he'd felt better.

The technical aspects of the mission had run like clockwork. The faxes had been received with outrage and hope, and the *Times'* crew had shuttled the video feed to news sources around the globe. But finally—as was the plan—the story had taken on a life of its own.

CNN had given it a name and a musical theme. So had FOX. They'd taken to calling Vince and the others heroes and investigations were sprouting like weeds.

The suicide of Senator Raines was huge, but now that he was gone it seemed as if every other politico in the country had something horrible to say about him—especially the ones being arrested.

It was going to take years for this to be resolved, what with court cases, international inquiries, evidence gathering and then there was the disposal of the gas. That worried him the most. They were still debating how to get rid of VX, and that had been going on since the seventies.

It was all of it terrible and wonderful, and he had thanked Corky Baker a hundred times today. He hoped, wherever he was, he knew that his story hadn't ended with his death.

The oddest thing though were all the requests for interviews. World renowned journalists were fighting each other to get at him. He supposed it was a compliment, but he'd never wanted to be part of the story, just to report it.

The boss, and not just the editor but the publisher, president and CEO, had given him the exclusive. After the story had run in the *Times*, then he would be free to discuss the particulars with other reporters. Hell, he had his own assistant whose sole job was to make sure he wasn't disturbed.

Of course, his parents had called, kvelling like he'd cured cancer. He hadn't, but damn it, what he had done was important. He'd helped save countless lives. He'd taken down an evil man, way before he'd become President. And he'd helped clear the names of nine incredibly brave people.

It was hard to hold all of what happened in his head. He was just a cub reporter. Someone who had to pick up the trash of those even slightly up the ladder. So, yeah, it made sense that he was stunned.

But the real shocker was he was still alive. With all the guns and weapons and clandestine phone calls, and the equipment and meeting forgers, he'd been convinced he wouldn't have lived past yesterday. Of course he'd carried on as if no one was after him, but damn. He was alive. And he was in debt up to his eyeballs.

How the hell was he going to pay for the goddamn Porsche? Or that stupid apartment, with the slippery sofa? He'd bought a watch he didn't need, clothes that made him uncomfortable. He'd bought silverware that cost a hundred and thirty dollars a serving.

His parents were going to kill him.

"Eli?"

He turned to his brand-new assistant, Gretchen. She was even greener than he was, but she was nice. "Yeah?"

"There's someone here to see you." She nodded toward the waiting room.

There were lots of people there, mostly reporters, but Gretchen couldn't mean them. They'd been around since the moment the story broke. "Who?"

"See that woman? The blonde? She says she knows you. That you went to high school together."

His heart sped up as he considered that it might be Janice. That she'd seen the news and suddenly her boyfriend wasn't looking so hot. But the only blonde out there was a little on the round side, wearing a skirt that was way the hell too short. She turned around, and he swallowed really hard. It was Janice. Only, she wasn't anything like he remembered.

She appeared about ten years older than she should have, and the hair he'd dreamt about for years looked like straw. Her lips, those perfect lips, were painted a bright, bright red.

She saw him and started waving hysterically, pushing the reporters away so she could come his way.

It was like one of those commercials, where the two

lovers run together in slow motion across a field of daisies. Only there weren't any flowers. And they weren't lovers. And it might have been better for everyone involved if he had been shot.

IT WAS ALMOST THREE WHEN they reached the Renegade. The calls had been made, tears had been wept. The most painful thing of all for Nate was talking to Cade's parents. He wasn't ashamed he'd cried bitter tears. Cade shouldn't have died.

He'd also called Corky Baker's wife. He wanted her to understand the role her husband had played. She'd asked if he'd like to come to dinner so he could tell their son. He told her he'd get back to her and that he'd like to meet her son. And that Vince would be with him.

He'd also spoken to the director of the FBI. As he'd expected, the director wanted all of them in Washington ASAP. Nate wouldn't tell them their location, but he gave his word they'd be in Las Vegas by eight o'clock that night. There would be a plane waiting.

Nate informed him that one member of the team would be delayed. He explained about Tam's parents. The director wasn't thrilled, but he could see there was no room for negotiation. He told Nate that Tam would have a plane ticket to San Francisco waiting for her at the terminal.

The bar was pretty empty, but he still looked around to see if Rodney was there. It was a dump, but he didn't give a damn. There were cold beers, a pretty decent television above the bar and his team was free.

He'd never been so proud of any unit he'd commanded. These people had shown fortitude and honor and a determination that was outside of most people's experience. He hoped each one of them wrote a book and got a million bucks for it. He didn't want them to experience any more hardships, financial or otherwise.

The real miracle of all of this was that in the midst of hell, almost all of them had found something great. Something bigger than Omicron, than politics. Love.

They sat at a big long ranch-house table. Vince asked if they had any chilled champagne, but he'd just gotten a look from the bartender that said loud and clear he'd be lucky to find imported beer.

Everyone ordered, and when the beers came, Nate stood. They all got quiet when he lifted his bottle. "It's been an honor serving with you," he said. "All of you. You were handed a lousy deal, but you played it out till the end. And you won. To the heroes of Kosovo."

They touched each other's bottles, going purposefully around the table. And when it was time to drink, Seth said, "To Cade. I hope to hell he had a front row seat."

"Amen, brother," Boone said.

"Hey, check it out." Kate was looking at the television.

"Today's suicide of Senator Jackson Raines, and the disclosure of the manufacture and sale of illegal chemical weapons has caused shock waves not only in Washington, but around the world." Behind the reporter was a helicopter shot of the manufacturing plant. Next was a wide shot of Leland Ingram being led out of the plant in handcuffs.

"Raines is dead?" Christie asked.

"Coward." Nate had to tamp down his urge to shoot something as he watched the news unfold. "The bastard should have had to fry along with everyone else involved."

"I just hope the Feds got the pricks who did this to me," Seth said, touching his bandaged eye gingerly.

"I do, too." Harper kissed him on the forehead, about the only place he wasn't bruised.

"Personally," Boone added, "I want to know once and for all who okayed our participation in this whole goddamned thing. Someone had to know. Someone in Delta."

"We'll find out." Nate had already decided that was going to be his first piece of business in D.C. "I won't rest until it happens."

"Did anyone call Eli?" Vince asked.

When no one stepped forward, he swore, then got out his cell phone. Vince had to shout to be heard, so he walked out of the bar, telling Eli to hold on.

Kate watched him leave, and Nate wondered how the two of them were going to make out now that the mission was over. Not the work part, that he knew. But the relationship.

He looked around the table at the men and women he'd come to know so well. All of them had found someone important, someone who made the fight bearable, but now? Would it all last past the hearings?

He looked at Tam and he thought about all they'd been through together. And how he'd come to need her. He didn't believe for a minute that time away would change a thing, at least not for him.

"Hey," he said, touching her arm.

She turned and smiled at him. As always, that smile alone was enough to knock his socks off.

"Come outside for a minute."

She didn't ask why, she just went with him, and when he touched her on the small of her back, she leaned into him to let him know his touch was more than welcome.

It was quiet outside, except for Vince shouting into his cell phone. Nate led her around to the side of the building. The view sucked. A small grocery store, a bunch of old cars and a billboard advertising the Virgin River Hotel in Mesquite. But he didn't look at any of that. All he wanted to see was Tam.

"So what are you going to do when you get home?" he asked. "Aside from taking care of your folks."

She sighed and rested her butt on the hood of an old Chevy. "Try to make sense of this. I'm not the person I was when I accepted that job offer. It feels as though it's been a hundred years since then."

Nate nodded, understanding perfectly.

"I'm pretty sure I still want to be a biochemist. But I'm terrified that I'll make another horrible mistake."

"First of all, it wasn't a mistake. You were lied to by people you had every right to believe would tell you the truth."

"Ah," she said, "but you're forgetting that I didn't go to Kosovo for some noble cause. I went because I wanted the money."

"That's not a sin, either."

"Maybe not in your book."

"Not in anyone's. Besides, you did some incredible work once you did find out what was going on. I doubt there's another scientist out there who could have put together those notes and come up with an antidote. Okay, maybe Stephen Hawking."

She laughed. "He's a quantum physicist."

Nate touched her chin. "But I got you to laugh."

She looked into his eyes, and he wondered what she saw there. Did she get that he had fallen for her? "You know, I'm not the guy I was, either."

"I know," she said. "You've got gray hair now."

"What?" He touched his head. "I do not."

She laughed again. "Uh-huh. At the temples. But don't worry, you look very distinguished."

"I don't want to look distinguished. I want to look hot."

That really cracked her up. She laughed so hard he couldn't help but join in, and it took them both a good while to calm back down. "Don't sweat it, soldier. You're still a hottie. I'm sure all the women in Washington will be lining up to show you the sights."

"I don't want that. Not anymore."

Her smile got a little crooked. "We'll see."

"Tam, you don't get it. I've found what I want."

"I know you believe that. For what it's worth, I hope it's true. I hope we go back to the real world and find out we're a match made in heaven."

"But?"

"It's only a hypothesis. We'll just have to wait and see the evidence."

"You brainiacs always have the most crackpot ideas."

"I'm right, and you know it."

"You realize they're not going to let you go. You will have to testify in Washington."

She nodded. "I know. I just want to get my folks settled. I'm hoping I don't have to leave them too soon."

"Will you stay with me? When you come?"

"I'd like to say I don't know, but I'm so weak when it comes to you. So yes, I probably will."

"Good."

"I don't want to make another mistake, Nate. Frankly, I couldn't handle it."

"All right. I won't push it. But don't be surprised if I call you every night until you figure things out."

"I'll be sad if you don't."

He leaned over and kissed her. "Don't be sad. I don't want you to be sad ever again."

She cupped his face with her small hands. "We've been through everything but the real stuff. Let's both focus on that, and then we'll know."

He nodded. "Whatever you say."

"I say let's get back to the others. We need this bit of downtime, don't you think? To be all together?"

"So smart. And so pretty. How do you do that?"

She blushed. "Kate was right. You are a charmer."

"Hey, you guys."

They turned to find Vince standing at the corner of the building. "Eli's famous."

Nate gave Tam one last private look, then he put his hands in his pockets as they went to join Vince. "Yeah?"

"He's getting his own byline and an exclusive first shot at the story. It was a very big deal at the *Times*."

"I'll bet," Nate said, grinning at how pleased Vince was.

"And all the other reporters want interviews with him. He's going to be on CNN tonight."

"Well," Tam said. "I hope this gets him laid."

Both men stopped and looked at each other, then at Tam. As she walked back into the bar, she was still grinning.

IT WAS GETTING LATE. Time to head back to Vegas and the media circus that was bound to greet them. Boone and Christie had gotten Milo, who'd been given special dispensation to come inside the bar, once the bartender realized he was hosting celebrities. Boone kept slipping the dog pretzels, and Christie kept slapping his hand.

They would leave the trucks at the airport, and it was anyone's guess if they'd ever retrieve them. Tam thought about the computers in that old apartment building. The hard drives had been wiped clean, but they could be used again, if someone wanted to load an operating system. Vince had bought that generator, and they'd only used it for one day. Some camper was going to get real lucky.

She turned to Vince. "How much money did you spend on all this?"

"Too much. I'm sending each one of you a bill."

"Seriously, are you going to be okay?"

"Better than you deadbeats." He turned to Nate. "While we're in D.C., why don't we find out if the government will pick up any of the tab. After all, we were doing their job for them."

"Great idea. Think we need to bring one of those canisters of dry ice to convince them?"

"Speaking of jobs," Vince said, ignoring Nate's joke completely, "remember how we were talking about starting up a security firm? How's that sitting with everyone now?"

"I'm in," Seth said. "What else am I gonna do?" He held up his claw. "I'm not the able-bodied man I once was."

"Count me in, too," Boone said. He turned to Christie. "We talked about it a lot. As long as Christie can work with us."

"I'm going back to the clinic," Harper said. "Sorry."

"You'll need someone to handle the money," Kate said. "And I am a CPA."

They were all looking at Nate, now. He grinned. "So we'll call it Pratchett Security?"

That caused a decent row. Enough so Tam had to shout when she looked up at the television screen. "Quiet, all of you. Look."

They did. It was a press conference and the man behind the podium was the chairman, Joint Chiefs of Staff. Next to him was the secretary of defense. The chairman was talking, and behind him were pictures of Nate, Cade, Boone and Seth in uniform.

Tam listened to the speech, but she watched the men as they listened intently to the chairman recount their battles and victories. He talked about how their courage and fortitude exemplified the best of what America and American soldiers stand for. How it was a travesty of justice that a U.S. senator could have branded them traitors, and that from this moment forward, the record would be set straight.

At that, she saw Nate's eyes fill with tears, and she knew if she looked, she'd see the same thing had happened to Seth and Boone.

When the chairman declared them national heroes, the press room gave them a standing ovation. That's when the tears slipped down Nate's cheeks. And her own.

# *18*

NATE SAT IN THE BACK of the limo staring at his cell phone. After two long months of interviews, depositions, debriefings and reports, he'd had it with Washington. They all had. It was time to start living a real life, and for Nate that meant Tam.

She'd been asked to come to D.C., and she'd informed the powers that be that they could all kiss her gorgeous ass, she was staying with her parents until they were completely well and settled back into their home. Okay, so maybe he'd added the gorgeous part, but her message had been so intractable that the powers and their minions had given up and gone to interview her.

Brava and all that, but damn it, he'd wished she'd come. He missed her more than he'd ever believed possible.

His cell rang, making him jump, but it wasn't a surprise call from Tam, but a check-in from his sister. "Hi, Christie."

"You need to come to dinner with us."

"I told you before, I don't want to go out to dinner."

"Too bad. You need to come to dinner with us."

He sat back on the cool leather, stretching his neck to release some tension. Today had been a particularly hellish experience. He'd been talking to Congress. Congress hadn't listened very well. "We'll do something tomorrow night, okay? I promise."

"No, it's not okay. Pay attention. You need to come to dinner."

"What's going on, Christie?"

"You'll find out *at dinner.*"

"Jesus, you're a pain in the ass."

"Seven-thirty, at Café Milano."

He groaned. "I wanted to get into a pair of jeans and order a pizza for the room."

"You can still have pizza. Just dress up a little."

"All right. But it better be worth it."

She'd hung up, of course. No one much wanted to be around him these days. Certainly not for a real dinner. It must be important.

He closed his eyes, wishing he were anywhere but here. And that was a lie, too. He wished he were with Tam. That's all. Didn't matter where.

It had started out well. He'd managed to call her every night, the time difference making that easier. But as the weeks had gone by the lawyers and politicians and just the general bullshit had gotten to him. Had he actually thought ending things with Omicron would make him a free man?

He'd come home with killer headaches and primed for fighting, and even over the phone Tam hadn't put up with that for long. Not that he blamed her, but damn it, she was the real light at the end of the daily tunnel.

They still spoke, but it was less frequent and the conversations were brief.

At least her parents were well on the mend. Her father still had the cast on his leg, but he'd walk again. Her mother was up and about and doting on Tam.

She'd been so worried about her reputation. He'd tried to tell her she'd be fine. Fine wasn't the half of it. She'd been offered research positions at the CDC, the World Health Organization and a post back at MIT. They all wanted her, lauded her in the journals and newspapers as brilliant. Most agreed there were only a few people in the world who could have come up with a working antidote under her circumstances.

That was his Tam. Only, he wasn't so sure she was his Tam anymore.

The limo kept inching its way through the rain and the traffic as his headache worsened. He fished the bottle of aspirin out of his pocket, and took a bottle of water from the bar. He swallowed three pills, hoping like hell they would do the trick.

He wanted this crap to be over. Finished. There were at least two more weeks left of congressional hearings, and after that, if they were lucky, the lawyers would be done with them, too.

At least the truth was out there. In every paper and on every TV set. Raines had left behind an enormous fortune, a reclusive wife and a journal that had half of Washington and California scared to death.

Ingram was in jail. His bail had been set at four million dollars, but since all his assets had been frozen, he wasn't going anywhere.

Because he'd given up the account in the Caymans, they'd been able to get the money and put it in a trust fund. Given the speed things happened in this town, he figured it would double in interest before they doled it out.

Finally, they were at the Watergate, and a uniformed kid with a big umbrella had opened his door. Given the time, he'd have about a half hour until he had to leave again. He made arrangements with the driver, and headed up to his suite.

At least they'd put him and his team up in style. They all had suites here and it wasn't uncommon to find Boone or Seth or Kate in the elevator on the way to Congress in the mornings. He loved them all like his family, but it would be good to go back to L.A. and find a house to call his own. Well, apartment at least. He wanted to live in Pasadena, if he could find a place he could afford.

The Army was giving them all their back pay, and that would really help. But it wouldn't be enough to buy a place and get the new business started.

He made his way up to his room, and he didn't stop until he was under the hottest shower he could stand.

"WE CAN'T DO THIS NOW," Kate said, putting her hands on top of Vince's. It was a pity, too, because this whole week had been hellish and they'd hardly had any sex at all.

He was sitting on the bed and she was standing in front of him. He put his head on her tummy and whimpered. "Don't make me go."

"We have to. We promised."

"I'm tired. There's a game on tonight. I don't want to wear a jacket."

"Too bad, too bad, too bad. It's not as if we have to do this every night."

He looked up at her. "No, we have to do it every day. And there are always reporters. And people who want to tell us things. And lawyers."

She petted his dark hair. "Ah, my poor sweetie. Does the big bad ex-homicide detective need his blankie?" She grinned, but only for a second. He pinched her butt. Hard. "Hey."

"Blankie, my ass."

"No, that was my ass."

"And a delectable ass it is. Can't we stay home and play with it?"

She lifted his head with a hand on each cheek. "I love you to pieces, but get up and get dressed. We can't be late."

His glower made her giggle as she went back to the bathroom to finish putting on her makeup. She had a sneaking suspicion what tonight was all about, but she couldn't be sure. She had high hopes, though.

"How come I don't have any bling for the claw?" Seth asked, studying it in the bathroom mirror. It was shiny for the most part and intimidating, which he liked. "Maybe a little somethin' somethin' would be, you know…"

Harper smacked him on the ass. "What I know is that white boys like you shouldn't be throwing around the terms bling and somethin' somethin'."

"Hey."

"I'm just saying."

He looked at her standing behind him, her hair its usual beautiful mess, her eyes alive with trouble. She was ready to go in a slinky black dress that was very low cut, and very sexy. She also had on a pair of silver earrings. "See?" he said, pointing at her. "You get to look all shiny and stuff."

"Tell you what," she said. "After dinner, we'll go find a tattoo parlor. They'll pierce your ears and I'll let you borrow all of my earrings."

He turned around and captured her. "Let's stay home and do unspeakable things to each other."

Harper sighed. "I wish."

"Come on. We'll say we were trapped in the elevator and couldn't get out."

"Honey, everyone's staying here. They'd know."

"Shit."

She kissed him. "Let's go, gorgeous. Even without the jewelry, you are so stunning every woman in D.C. wants to have your little soldiers."

He laughed all the way to the door, and then some.

BOONE SAT AT THE HEAD OF the table with Christie on his right. He knew she was looking forward to the evening, so he hadn't said anything when she'd wanted to leave twenty minutes early. To tell the truth, he was looking forward to it, too. They'd been under the gun for so damn long. They might not be hunted anymore, but they weren't left alone, either.

It had taken a toll on all of them, but Nate had been hit the hardest. And because Christie loved her brother, she'd been worried sick. That, and the fact that she'd had to board her beloved Milo had kept her on edge since they'd arrived in D.C.

He'd ordered a beer. Café Milano had this big famous wine cellar, but damn it, he liked beer. Christie had stuck with water, although it was sparkling.

She looked at her watch again.

"Honey, they'll be here soon, okay. Everything's all set. Why don't you try to relax?"

Her brows furrowed, he could tell she wanted to tell him to go take a flying leap. Instead, she took his hand in hers. "I love you."

"I love you, too."

"No. I mean it. I love you. I hate that we had to go through all this crap, but I'm so, so glad I found you."

He laughed a little, wondering what was going on. "Is everything okay?"

"Yeah, why?"

He looked down at their hands, where she was gripping him so hard her fingers were white.

"Oh."

He leaned over and gave her a kiss that honestly didn't belong in public. "I'm crazy about you, too," he said. "So much, I'm going to let you go so you can talk to your brother."

She spun around to see Nate behind her. Boone didn't even feel insulted when she dropped his hand like yesterday's news and rushed over to hug him. Well, maybe just a little. He just couldn't help wondering what was at the bottom of all this, and who the extra seat was for. Christie was up to something. He just hoped it wouldn't end up coming back to bite her.

NATE COUNTED THE CHAIRS, and he couldn't help the lump in his throat. Who else could Christie have invited? He'd talked to Tam yesterday and she hadn't said a word, but a surprise? That felt like something Christie would do.

She followed his gaze, and put her hand up to her mouth. "Oh, God. I just— I'm sorry, Nate. It's not Tam. Damn me for a fool, I didn't even think."

He smiled to hide his disappointment. "That's okay. I didn't really expect it. So who's the mystery guest?"

"It's good, I promise. Not as good as Tam, I know, but still. I think you'll be happy."

He kissed the top of her head. "I'm sure I will be. Now, where's the booze?"

"I think Boone already ordered you a beer."

He sat across from Christie, and tried to participate as the others arrived. He really had no appetite, but he ordered some pasta which he figured he could push around his plate. The food came, and still there was that empty seat.

Christie wasn't saying a word, despite the haranguing by the rest of them. Finally, just after the table was cleared, someone they all knew walked in the door.

It was Judge Andrew Petit. He wasn't involved in the Omicron case—at least not officially—but he was famous as hell. He ended up on television more often than Larry King. Often on Larry King. His outrage about Omicron and Senator Raines had been vocal and consistent. He'd written Op-Ed pieces for the *Washington Post* and the *New York Times*, rallying those who had a stake in this to make sure it could never happen again.

He was young for a judge, and had a reputation as a ladies' man, but tonight he'd come solo. He shook hands all around and finally sat down in the empty seat.

Christie was grinning like a fool, and for the life of him, Nate couldn't put the two things together. What secret could she share with the judge?

A moment after he'd been seated, three waiters came to the table bearing some damned expensive bottles of champagne. Glasses were filled, but nothing was said until they were left to themselves.

"I assume Ms. Pratchett hasn't told you the news."

"No, she hasn't," Harper said. "And frankly, it's pissing us off."

Judge Petit laughed, and sat back in his wooden chair as if he was about to give a ruling. "Something unusual was brought to my attention three weeks ago. Mr. Eldridge, the attorney representing Omicron International has also been retained by Mrs. Raines. As you know, her late husband left a considerable personal fortune."

Nate looked at Seth, then Boone, but they seemed just as confused as he was.

"Mrs. Raines has asked me to distribute a great deal of that fortune to the individuals who were dealt with so maliciously by her late husband. That's all of you, Dr. Chen, and the estate of Charles Dugan, or Cade, as you've been calling him."

"How much of a fortune are we talking about?" Kate asked.

The judge picked up his glass and smiled. "Each of you will receive six million dollars. Unfortunately, we couldn't convince Uncle Sam to make it tax free, but still, it will be some considerable recompense for what's happened."

"Judge, I appreciate this, believe me, but what about the people Raines killed? The families of those in Serbia and Chad?"

"They will also receive reparation, but this is a private matter, not one to go through the courts. I'm involved as a personal favor, and believe me, it's my pleasure to be able to give you the news."

Nate turned to Christie. "When did you find out about all this?"

"Yesterday. See?" she said. "I told you it was good."

"Ladies and gentlemen, may I offer a toast?" Petit stood. "I hope this gives you all security for a future you all so richly deserve. It's not enough, not by a mile, but it'll help. And, I'm sure, it will help Mrs. Raines sleep better at night. To the future."

Nate sipped his champagne, but he wasn't awash in glee. Yes, the money would be good. It would help him get the house in Pasadena and it would be a good-size cushion for the new security business. But it felt hollow. Too little, too late.

They'd all been through hell, and no amount of money would give them back the years they'd lost. He supposed he'd feel better about it if he and Tam...

"Mr. Pratchett."

Petit was standing by his chair. Nate rose. "Thanks for delivering the news yourself," Nate said, holding out his hand.

Petit shook it. "I haven't had a chance to thank you personally. Oddly, you've restored my faith in the

United States armed forces. If they've got men like you, we're all in good hands."

"Thank you, sir. But they don't have me any longer."

"That's fine. You've done more than your share. I know the hearings are draining, but they'll be over soon."

"Not soon enough."

Petit laughed.

"One thing," Nate said, stopping him before he moved over to Boone. "Has anyone notified Dr. Chen?"

"That's all been taken care of. I'm sure she's been made aware, as have the Dugan family."

"Thanks."

Nate sat down and went back to his beer. He wanted to be more excited, but all he could think of was that he hadn't even been able to bring the news to Tam.

BY THE TIME HE WALKED BACK into his hotel suite, Nate couldn't wait to fall into bed. He resented the time it would take to undress, to brush his damn teeth.

He shut the door and headed back to his bedroom, peeling off his jacket as he went. It hit the floor, and his shoes came off as he unbuttoned his shirt.

His fingers froze when he saw her. She was standing by the bed, and she looked nervous and happy all at the same time. He wasn't even sure she was real until she walked over to him, touched his cheeks with her small palm and said, "I couldn't stand it another day. Not another minute. I love you, I miss you and I don't want to be anywhere without you."

He had her in his arms the next second, and he kissed

her hard as he lifted her right off the floor. It wasn't easy, the kissing part, because he was laughing, and so was she, and neither one of them was breathing all that well.

He ended up putting her down on the bed. He sat next to her, touching her arm, her hair, her smooth cheek.

"So, you're okay that I'm here?"

He laughed. "What do you think?"

"I think I've had plenty of time to figure out what I want. I'm taking a job at UCLA."

"You're rich now. You're still going to work?"

She nodded. "I know you are."

"Yeah. I don't do leisure all that well."

"Really? Then I guess I'll have to teach you a thing or two."

"Oh?"

She was touching him, too. His knee, his arm, his shoulder. "I want us to go somewhere. Tahiti or Alaska or Switzerland. Somewhere we can be alone. Where we can stay in the room for a week if we feel like it. I need time to decompress, and I know you do, too. What do you think?"

He leaned over and kissed her again, and this time he was in no rush. When he finally pulled back so that he could get this gorgeous woman in bed, she said, "I'm taking that as a yes."

"Tam, you can ask me any damn thing you want, and the answer's going to be exactly that."

"Oh, really?" She looked him over from his still half-buttoned shirt to his black socks. "Interesting."

"Oh, yeah," he said. "By the way. I love you, too."

She smiled. "I know. Now, let's you and me lock and load."

\* \* \* \* \*

*Turn the page for a sneak preview of*
*IF I'D NEVER KNOWN YOUR LOVE*
*by*
*Georgia Bockoven*

*From the brand-new series*
**HARLEQUIN EVERLASTING LOVE.**
*Every great love has a story to tell.* ™

*One year, five months and four days missing.*

There's no way for you to know this, Evan, but I haven't written to you for a few months. Actually, it's been almost a year. I had a hard time picking up a pen once more after we paid the second ransom and then received a letter saying it wasn't enough. I was so sure you were coming home that I took the kids along to Bogotá so they could fly home with you and me, something I swore I'd never do. I've fallen in love with Colombia and the people who've opened their hearts to me. But fear is a constant companion when I'm there. I won't ever expose our children to that kind of danger again.

I'm at a loss over what to do anymore, Evan. I've begged and pleaded and thrown temper tantrums with every official I can corner both here and at home. They've been incredibly tolerant and understanding, but in the end as ineffectual as the rest of us.

I try to imagine what your life is like now,

what you do every day, what you're wearing, what you eat. I want to believe that the people who have you are misguided yet kind, that they treat you well. It's how I survive day to day. To think of you being mistreated hurts too much. If I picture you locked away somewhere and suffering, a weight descends on me that makes it almost impossible to get out of bed in the morning.

Your captors surely know you by now. They have to recognize what a good man you are. I imagine you working with their children, telling them that you have children, too, showing them the pictures you carry in your wallet. Can't the men who have you understand how much your children miss you? How can it not matter to them?

How can they keep you away from us all this time? Over and over, we've done what they asked. Are they oblivious to the depth of their cruelty? What kind of people are they that they don't care?

I used to keep a calendar beside our bed next to the peach rose you picked for me before you left. Every night I marked another day, counting how many you'd been gone. I don't do that any longer. I don't want to be reminded of all the days we'll never get back.

When I can't sleep at night, I tell you about my day. I imagine you hearing me and smiling over the details that make up my life now. I never tell you how defeated I feel at moments or how hard I work to hide it from everyone for fear they will see it as a reason to stop believing you are coming home to us.

And I couldn't tell you about the lump I found in my breast and how difficult it was going through all the tests without you here to lean on. The lump was benign—the process reaching that diagnosis utterly terrifying. I couldn't stop thinking about what would happen to Shelly and Jason if something happened to me.

We need you to come home.

I'm worn down with missing you.

I'm going to read this tomorrow and will probably tear it up or burn it in the fireplace. I don't want you to get the idea I ever doubted what I was doing to free you or thought the work a burden. I would gladly spend the rest of my life at it, even if, in the end, we only had one day together.

You are my life, Evan.

I will love you forever.

\* \* \* \* \*

*Don't miss this deeply moving*
**HARLEQUIN EVERLASTING LOVE** *story*
*about a woman's struggle to bring back*
*her kidnapped husband from Colombia and*
*her turmoil over whether to let go, finally,*
*and welcome another man into her life.*
*IF I'D NEVER KNOWN YOUR LOVE*
*by Georgia Bockoven*
*is available March 27, 2007.*

*And also look for*
*THE NIGHT WE MET*
*by Tara Taylor Quinn,*
*a story about finding love*
*when you least expect it.*

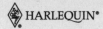

# HARLEQUIN® *Romance*®

*presents a brand-new trilogy by*

# PATRICIA THAYER

*Rocky Mountain*
# BRIDES

**Three sisters come home to wed.**

**In April don't miss**

# *Raising the Rancher's Family,*

*followed by*

## *The Sheriff's Pregnant Wife,*

*on sale May 2007,*

**and**

## *A Mother for the Tycoon's Child,*

*on sale June 2007.*

## Romantic
# SUSPENSE

### Excitement, danger and passion guaranteed!

*USA TODAY* bestselling author
**Marie Ferrarella**
is back with the second installment
in her popular miniseries,
*The Doctors Pulaski: Medicine
just got more interesting...*
DIAGNOSIS: DANGER is on sale
April 2007 from Silhouette®
Romantic Suspense (formerly
Silhouette Intimate Moments).

*Look for it wherever
you buy books!*

# REQUEST YOUR FREE BOOKS!

**2 FREE NOVELS
PLUS 2
FREE GIFTS!**

 HARLEQUIN®

 *Blaze*®

**Red-hot reads!**

HB07

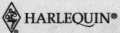

# HARLEQUIN®

# Blaze™

## COMING NEXT MONTH

**#315 COMING UNDONE Stephanie Tyler**
There's a bad boy in camouflage knocking at Carly Winters's door, and she knows she's in trouble. The erotic fax that Jonathon "Hunt" Huntington's waving in her face—she can explain; how the buff Navy SEAL got ahold of it—she can't. But she sure wants to find out!

**#316 SEX AS A SECOND LANGUAGE Jamie Sobrato**
*Lust in Translation, Bk. 1*
Ariel Turner's sexual tour of Europe has landed her in Italy seeking the perfect Italian lover. But despite the friendliness of the locals, she's not having much luck. Until the day the very hot Marc Sorrella sits beside her. Could it be she's found the ideal candidate?

**#317 THE HAUNTING Hope Tarr**
*Extreme*
History professor Maggie Holliday's new antebellum home has everything she's ever wanted—including the ghost of Captain Ethan O'Malley, a Union soldier who insists Maggie's the reincarnation of his lost love. And after one incredibly sexual night in his arms, she's inclined to believe him....

**#318 AT HIS FINGERTIPS Dawn Atkins**
*Doing it...Better! Bk. 3*
When a fortune-teller predicts the return of a man from her past, Esmeralda McElroy doesn't expect Mitch Margolin. The sexy sizzle is still between them, but he's a lot more cautious than she remembers. Does this mean she'll have to seduce him to his senses?

**#319 BAD BEHAVIOR Kristin Hardy**
*Sex & the Supper Club II, Bk. 3*
Dominick Gordon can't believe it. He thinks his eyes are playing tricks on him when he spots the older, but no less beautiful, Delaney Phillips—it's been almost twenty years since they dated as teenagers. Still, Dom's immediate feelings show he's all man, and Delaney's all woman....

**#320 ALL OVER YOU Sarah Mayberry**
*Secret Lives of Daytime Divas, Bk. 2*
The last thing scriptwriter Grace Wellington wants is for the man of her fantasies to step into her life. But Mac Harrison, in his full, gorgeous glory, has done exactly that. Worse, they're now working together. That is, if Grace can keep her hands to herself!

**www.eHarlequin.com**

HBCNM0307